What Became of Lumerso?
Javier Ángel

Finalist
VIII International Novel Contest
Contacto Latino

ISBN-13: 978-1-63065-134-3

PUKIYARI PUBLISHERS
www.pukiyari.com

I dedicate this book to Jesus and Armando,
without them this novel
wouldn't have been possible.

Table of Contents

Epilogue

Mexico, Mexico City, 2019

The sun reflects its light on a wall. Walls painted in a black color divide the space. An empty room can be found on the first floor. At the end of a dark hallway, a bathtub with no water. A yellowed white curtain separates it from the sink. A man cleans his buttocks with water from the toilet. Others move from one room to another. The lazy wind hits an aluminum sheet while a tree trunk holds it to keep it from flying off. There's no electricity today. A Juan Gabriel ballad comes from the hoarse speaker of a cellphone. Two rooms to the right, two more to the left. Moaning. Leaking of disgusting dark water dampens the black couch. Slowly, the smoke of cigarettes creates a thick fog filling the whole floor. It's impossible to see a thing. A naked man exits one room and enters the terrace. Another hallway leads to three spaces the size of a closet, a second one leads to nowhere. In the last floor there are several bedrooms with bunkbeds. Vinyl pads reek of aged bodily fluids, layers of vomit, rotten garbage and stale smoke. You can hear moaning coming from the rooms. Anxious bodies, apathetic bodies, tense bodies, bodies lacking desire. It could be any time of the day: maybe dawn or noon or the evening. Lumerso hears the doorbell ring, he knows someone's coming. He cannot find any place to hide. All the bedrooms are occupied. He hates the light coming in through the terrace. He never dares to get closer. The light extends, covering half the wall, until it disappears on the other patio. He'd like to touch someone. Feel anyone one more time. Find himself once again with that warmth of someone else's body. He goes down into the basement, sometimes he can close his eyes there. A cross from the time of the viceroyalty hangs in the wrong place. The basement is occupied already. It always is. That's where the sounds come from, bodies manhandling one another, whispers, sighs. Someone squeals or perhaps he's crying. Is that odor saliva or is it semen? Three or four men are inside. Lumerso cannot stand that stench of dampness, of sweat, of filth. He cannot tolerate having to smell it every day. Cannot tell if those scents are coming from the humans or the opossums that also inhabit that place. Yesterday he saw a cat. He would've liked to have it as a pet. As a child he had a dog, but now it's all the same to him, whether it's a cat, an iguana, or a pig, as long as he can have it near him. The cat with yellow eyes stares at him for a long while before running off and reaching the roof of the terrace. Lumerso knows he cannot go up there.

He moves on through the staircase until he reaches the landing that separates the two mansions. He likes thinking that the house is his, that no one else occupies that space. High ceilings, endless down-slopes and several steps going upwards lead to labyrinths with no way out. The place seems to have its own sound. Sometimes he listens and it's as if the house speaks to him, as if it has stories to tell him. He lies down on the floor trying to decipher what it says. He imagines a family from the time of Porfirio Diaz returning home after Midnight Mass on Christmas Eve. He can almost see the children running and a brand-new Christmas tree standing right outside the entrance to the dining room. From there he can delight at the aromas of extraordinary dishes and a tasty cornbread sizzling out of the oven served with hot chocolate. The patriarch helping his children open their presents in the company of a woman knitting beside the fireplace. That makes him smile.

From a hole in the ceiling peeks another ray of light. Where before there was a kitchen, there are now two leather couches. At the back, a half-open cupboard door. Two mops at the sides of a man sitting on a stool. His eyes are reddened. The same as everyone else's when they arrive. The cheeks swollen and lips colored pink. He contemplates him. His hair flows down in ringlets. In a daze of desperation, or perhaps some sadness, he thinks how sweet it'd be to touch his hair with his fingers. Lumerso watches his chest and sees how his body hair tries to escape through the shirt. He wants to touch him, talk to him. Tell him he's good-looking, that there's no need for him to be in that place. The man stands holding his slightly erect penis. He walks until getting lost in the darkness. Another one that has just arrived follows him. Lumerso knows what's coming. It upsets him. He sees it all the time, at all hours. The light of a cellphone lights up their faces. He thinks that might be how it would be under a half moon. They kiss, suck, sniff each other like dogs. The one with the body hair sucks the penis of the new one. He enjoys it. They both do. Lumerso can tell when one pulls out a condom. The other begs. A symphony of moans can be heard.

Chapter I

Chapultepec Park, 2002

When he was just finishing elementary school,
Lumerso would ride his bike around the Chapultepec
Park before going to school. He loved getting up early
and pedaling all the way to the park or taking a dip in
the pool at the club. He enjoyed seeing how the first
rays of sunlight peeked between the leaves before
appearing radiantly over the trees. The beams of
sunshine seemed to play hide-and-seek behind the
clouds. Once he was surprised by how the clouds
formed penises of all sizes: large, medium, and small.
This caused him to get an erection. He slid his hand
inside his pants and touched his own dick. Then he
pulled his hand out, spat saliva on it, placed it back on
his penis and tugged on it several times until a soft,
clear, damp liquid soaked his hand and underpants. A
policeman on the sidewalk saw him. Lumerso ignored

his admonishing look and tugged on his phallus once more. He felt pride knowing he belonged to the group of grown-ups. That morning, as he lay on the grass to contemplate the clouds, he wanted to see if he could also find women's breasts. He found none.

He arrived home happy. Ate some *chilaquiles* that Jimena, the housemaid, served him and he offered the leftovers to Oliver, his dog, who wouldn't stop looking at him. He finished an English essay he was working on for school. Then he climbed back on his bicycle. He seemed to have all the energy in the world. That morning he thought of everything he might like to be as a grown-up: A movie star, a great economist, a radio host, or even the new President of Mexico and that way end, once and for all, all the corruption in the country.

Before making it to school, Lumerso met Edgar, his childhood friend. They rode down Nuevo Leon Avenue until they reached their school. During recess he took the chance to ask Edgar how many times a day he jacked off. Feeling ashamed, Edgar answered that his mother forbade him from doing such things because that would destroy his brain cells. Edgar also said that his mother was tired of trying to get rid of the stains on his sheets. Lumerso laughed. He said the whole issue of killing brain cells by masturbating were only tall tales from the grown-ups. He proposed that one day they should jerk off together, like they used to when they were younger, and then do some difficult math exercises to prove that they were still as intelligent as before. He told Edgar about what he did in the park.

"We should go riding together on Friday, that way we can also masturbate together and see whose has gotten bigger," Lumerso suggested.

Edgar replied that that was insane, that they'd be thrown into jail for being exhibitionists or sexual deviants. Lumerso answered that he meant that there was no one at the park on Friday after school, just one cop who patrolled every so often but Lumerso didn't believe the officer could really tell from far away what they would be doing. He told him he would always masturbate there, and no one ever saw him.

On Friday they chained their bicycles at the entrance to Chapultepec Park. They went for a run. After passing the statue of Don Quixote they went towards some bamboo trees by the riverside. Edgar was astonished at Lumerso's bold suggestion. He had no shame. If they got caught, they'd end up in the slammer. The policeman had just passed by, he wouldn't be returning for a while. Joggers kept running by, though nobody paid attention to what the friends started doing. Edgar saw Lumerso's penis and pulled his own out to measure them.

"Holy crap, asshole, it's much bigger than mine," Edgar pointed out.

Edgar closed his eyes. He forced himself to think about the breasts that were starting to show on Claudia, the blonde girl who moved to the city from Durango. Lumerso took the opportunity to start sucking him. Edgar said nothing. Instead, he kept visualizing Claudia and how lovely that little hole in between her butt cheeks would be by now. She would surely have body hair, just like him. He would kiss her everywhere before putting his 'willy' inside her. Lumerso kept sucking until he and Edgar came at the same time. They did it once before in Lumerso's house, but nothing happened. Neither of them wanted to talk about it. In silence, they walked to where their bikes were parked, they unchained them and took off without saying a word to each other.

The next Monday Edgar wasn't waiting for him outside his place. Lumerso rang the doorbell but no one answered. He went back to check on his bike. He was surprised to see his friend standing by Claudia. Edgar didn't want to look at him. They went to class without talking to each other. Lumerso felt as if he'd lost his best friend. Tuesday was the same. Edgar didn't wait for him. Lumerso showed up at his place without warning. They had some math and physics work they needed to finish. He decided to go see him. This time Edgar told him they'd work on the dining room table. They talked about the different solutions for the physics problems until midnight. Edgar said it was better to leave it there and that they had probably solved them all already.

"Are we friends?" Lumerso finally asked, as he stood up to leave.

It took Edgar several seconds to answer. Finally, in a careful tone he told him he wouldn't be sucking his dick again, that he didn't like that crap, that he should go suck some other asshole.

Magdalena, Edgar's mother, didn't like to go to sleep until her son did. She'd leave her door ajar to listen in on their conversations. That day she couldn't believe what she heard.

"Fine," Lumerso said angrily.

"You're always horny, dude," Edgar continued in a different tone.

The next morning Edgar went to school on his own. Lumerso didn't want to pick him up either. Even though they would see each other they wouldn't talk. Edgar kept going to school, until one day his mother went to pick him up. Two weeks passed, but Lumerso didn't see Edgar again. After class, he decided to stop at his place. Magdalena didn't want to let him in. With the door only half-opened she quickly explained that Edgar had earned a scholarship to study in Washington, D.C. and wouldn't be returning for a while. Lumerso didn't ask anymore. He rode his bike all the way to Mexico Park. There, he sat on the sidewalk, remembering everything they'd ever done together. He felt regret for asking him to go to Chapultepec that day. Lumerso wept like a little boy until a squirrel interrupted his crying. The animal was waiting for something to eat, and as it got no response, it climbed back up on its tree.

"If I'd had something to give you, you wouldn't have taken off, right?" Lumerso yelled, shaking from rage.

Two women who were sweeping looked at him and dismissed him as a madman. He got home and wrote his last diary entry about Edgar.

Chapter II

Acapulco, 2007

Sometimes Lumerso remembers the trip to Acapulco. That day the tide pulled him to the bottom of the ocean with such force that it almost drowned him. When he opened his eyes two men were pressing on his chest. A woman placed her mouth against his lips to save his life. Lumerso felt fear. He wondered if he might still have his ID in his pocket, or the money Garzo gave him. The woman looked at him for a moment. She squeezed his chest and his cheeks until Lumerso coughed and water came out of his mouth. It made him uncomfortable. He wanted to say thank you but felt embarrassed and left without uttering any words.

He met Garzo earlier behind some rocks in a gay beach in Acapulco. He never traveled alone before. He enjoyed doing whatever he wanted and not what others said he should do. Lumerso climbed on the rocks to get a tan. Several men were naked. Near the sea a *gringo* was giving a local oral sex. Lumerso wanted to get naked as well, he had nothing to hide. He quickly removed his bathing suit and then positioned himself facing down. His ass was the only white piece of that young, lightly tanned body. Several men stopped and try to start a conversation with him. Lumerso only smiled and stayed silent. Garzo was the exception. He looked at him from the distance before offering him a towel. Lumerso nodded with his head. Then he stood, covering his genitals, while Garzo placed a towel over the rock. In a friendly way Garzo asked if he needed sunscreen, or maybe a massage. Lumerso responded by flashing a sassy grin. He was in a good mood, earlier he had fish and two really big piña coladas. He wasn't used to drinking and the rum relaxed him. Garzo began rubbing coconut oil on his back, letting his fingers slide all the way down to the point of grazing his anus. Lumerso responded by bending his back a bit. Although, after what had happened in Cuernavaca he preferred to be the active one in bed, he enjoyed the touch of Garzo's fingers on his skin. When he finished rubbing his back, Garzo moved down to his butt cheeks, slowly making his way to Lumerso's testicles. He breathed in before pushing his tongue in between the cheeks. Lumerso spread his legs a bit more. He felt Garzo's saliva inside him.

The sun was beginning to hide behind the mountains. Different shades of an orange color painted the bay. Two voyeurs approached, wanting to participate. Garzo sent them packing right away. Lumerso wanted to look closely at the man enjoying him. He took off his glasses and stared at him. A semi-erect penis surprised Garzo. Then he gave Lumerso a hand job until he got a complete erection.

"I never thought…" Garzo stated, his eyes wide open.

"That it would be so big?" Lumerso interrupted.

Garzo chuckled before kissing him on the lips. They noticed they had new spectators. This time they didn't care. Garzo began to suck him. He enjoyed his phallus like it was a chocolate sundae. Lumerso pushed his head down until he babbled without first thinking over his words:

"This is gonna cost you!"

He immediately regretted what he'd just said. He had no money, nor did he know where he would sleep that night, but it wasn't a reason to begin charging strangers on the beach. Garzo pulled out a five-hundred pesos bill. He placed it over Lumerso's leg. Garzo kept sucking until Lumerso couldn't hold it anymore. He spattered all over the place what he'd so fervently kept restrained.

The next day they woke up smiling. Garzo fixed breakfast placing muffins, orange juice and coffee on the table. The heavy curtains concealed the lights of dawn on the other side of the room.

"You never told me what you're doing here," Lumerso asked while yawning.

"A medical conference," Garzo replied from the kitchen.

Lumerso thought he must have hit the jackpot with this man, who aside from paying him for the pleasure would give him lodging and food. He wouldn't have to worry about going back home. After all, his father loathed him, and he would have to make a new life for himself. All he had to do was learn to love Garzo. Though he liked him, he thought they both might benefit from the relationship. A bit later he decided he didn't want to think about it any longer.

"I'm leaving a thousand pesos for you to buy some provisions and the rest is for you," Garzo yelled before opening the door.

Stumbling, Lumerso ran from the bedroom before asking:

"Not saying goodbye with a kiss?"

"Don't steal anything. The flat isn't mine," Garzo remarked in a serious tone.

Upon closing the door, Lumerso thought that maybe he'd found the 'famous' love. It was like the stories of Grandma Victoria: he knew life's mysterious ways had gotten him there. What had happened in Cuernavaca was in the past. That horrendous moment wouldn't have to ruin the rest of his life. He savored once again the smell of Garzo on his fingers, his lips and even on the essence left on his penis. He felt like a different man and not like the brat who'd been forced to abandon his home. He took the keys Garzo left on the kitchen island and went back to the beach where they'd met the day before. He was quivering with happiness. He asked the waitress for some shrimp with garlic and a bucket of beers. He sprawled himself on a deckchair. Didn't want to talk to anyone. Then he decided to rent a jet ski and take it for a spin. After a short time, he grew bored. He walked towards the rocks. This time he didn't lay down. He remembered what he and Garzo had done the day before. It excited him to know that by sundown he'd feel his ass cheeks grazing his penis before penetrating him. He drank his last beer.

He wanted to swim to the rock where the fishermen kept the mussels during the night dew. It was the eve of a full moon. The tide was starting to rise. He didn't care. A hard wave returned him to the shore, pushed down his shorts, he wasn't wearing underclothes. He held his breath to get submerged again; but, this time, a second wave took him to the bottom, delivering a blow to his forehead. He lost consciousness. The waitress and two tourists pulled him from the water. That night Lumerso didn't want to return to Garzo. Having been so close to death made him change his mind. He remembered how far away his parents were, and his sister Julieta. The worst, he thought, would be to die there, without anyone who loved him by his side. He couldn't end his life in a beach far from home, far from his schoolmates. He took the bus back to Mexico City. Got home after midnight. This time, no one asked anything.

Remember the bay, the immensity of that sea. Remember the taste of the seafood, the beers and that man's kisses. Write your plans, like Grandma Victoria used to say, later God will make sure to erase them. After thinking it over, Lumerso put his head on the pillow and fell asleep.

Chapter III

Escandon Neighborhood, 2019

Close to him a man is crying, or maybe he's getting off, he seems to have found what he was looking for. Lumerso cannot distinguish between pleasure and pain anymore. The doorbell can be heard again. Some, like vultures, wait for fresh meat. Two men talk while resting against one of the handrails. A strong smell of marijuana permeates the place. Mumbling, laughing, and whispering can be heard in the distance. One is taken and manhandled by six others; they drag him to the basement. He's blindfolded. He's young, perhaps a couple of years younger than Lumerso. On the way there they take off his clothes. Leave him with underpants that only cover his penis. The skin of his ass is dark. A bearded man in a blue shirt carries a cellphone, he's recording. Another gets mad. He yells that if he keeps recording, he'll fuck him up.

The one in the blue shirt doesn't turn it off, but he slips the phone into his pocket. Other spectators follow them. They're the ones that like to look on, but do not participate. They become witnesses of what happens there; although, no one ever says anything. No one must know what happens in the basement. Married men, businessmen, entrepreneurial men that remove their fake masks to show their true identities. Blackmailing is uncommon. No one really gets to know anyone else. Men who do not mention what they do during lunchtime or before going back home. Men who look away when they run into someone they know. They know each other but wish they didn't. However, they are the only ones who know they were there. Their secret is safe.

They hang the young man between four bars, head up. One of his hands slips free, another man ties it immediately. They tear his underwear. The boy seems to enjoy it. He savors what he's sucking. He's licking furiously. He smells a liquid. They force him to. They take away his blindfold. Light-colored eyes turn to the front. He inhales again. With no lubrication a darker man penetrates him. He's not using a condom. The guy screams. Moans. They're all becoming excited. Together they sound exactly like a porno movie. They touch themselves. They want to be him, the one who penetrates, the one who sucks, the one being taken. They need someone to suck them too. While the darker one penetrates him, another climbs on top of him and pushes his penis. A scream bounces off everywhere. The moans multiply. Another pushes up his leg towards his neck. Now there's three of them. The third is suffocating him with his genitals. He shuts him up.

Forces him to eat his dick. The boy sucks frenetically until he bites. He cannot handle it anymore. The man strikes his face. Another responds by delivering a kick to his back. The other two keep moving their penises inside him. His face feels numb. The struggle becomes more and more savage. Some of the men leave the basement. Some others go down with their penises lubricated. Some form a line behind four more that wish to penetrate him. The young man hanging seems to be getting off again. He's been drugged. Cannot feel anymore. The new ones penetrate him while they swallow each other's tongues. The boy no longer feels or enjoys. He closes his eyes. Lumerso watches the young man lose consciousness. He waits. Gets closer to him, looks him in the eye, but he can see he's still there, awaiting.

Chapter IV

Juarez Neighborhood, 2010

That night Lumerso went out with Erick. In his pocket he had the pills prescribed for his mother's depression, plus two blue ones he bought at the Discount Pharmacy. He used them now with more frequency. Before leaving he told Julieta that the next day they'd go for a walk to the Marquesa, to eat the marrow soup they liked so much.

Erick wasn't Lumerso's boyfriend anymore, they broke up as a couple after four months but remained friends. They would still go dancing, or to have a drink on Saturdays. Lumerso would say he didn't like drugs, that he only did it to please Erick. Neither of them had finished college. Erick had a part-time job as a taxi driver. Lumerso worked answering calls in a customer service call center. Weekdays were difficult and annoying; and the earnings scant. Erick managed to sell cocaine and many other drugs in the many joints of the Zona Rosa. He insisted Lumerso should do it too. In response, Lumerso would tell him he rather earned a living doing something that wouldn't ruin him at such a young age. Erick tried all the drugs before selling them. At times he'd be found locked in the bathroom covered in his own vomit. After a few drinks and pills, Lumerso took off to sell his body in Hamburgo Street. It was what he knew how to do best, aside from the fact he felt fortunate being as hung as his father. He maintained several profiles in *Manhunt* and *Craigslist*, among other websites. He met up with many who quickly became regular clients, as he called them. Men from all socioeconomic classes in Mexico City. He was sought out by politicians, architects, doctors, and actors that would devastate the tender hearts of many followers of soap operas if they saw them in their preferred positions in bed. Some became his friends, others only used him for the pleasure of having someone they could chat with, go to the movies, or to enjoy his company.

When Lumerso searched crazily for Erick in the dive and didn't find him he decided to leave. It wasn't the first time he did it; besides, they'd agreed that they'd return home early that night. Angry as he was, Lumerso decided to take the rest of the pills. His head began to spin. A sharp pain in his neck tormented him. The blue pills were beginning to have an effect. He wanted to fuck. He left the place. Walked until he made it to the corner of Hamburgo and Praga streets. There he stood for ten minutes holding on to a Jetta parked on the street. Lumerso was incoherent. Between the alcohol and the pills, he couldn't articulate a thing. He held his penis and showed it as the only merchandise he could sell. A man with glasses and a long face asked him several questions before Lumerso climbed into the car. Three bills of a hundred was the agreement between the two. Lumerso closed his eyes, he wanted to sleep. The man told him he was there to work; that if he wanted to sleep, he would have been better off leaving him where he found him. Lumerso didn't answer, but he opened his eyes and kept them open. After driving for several minutes, they arrived at a hotel near Circuito Interior. The man tried to get Lumerso out of the car, but he'd fallen asleep already. The receptionist at the hotel left to go to the bathroom after the man had paid for the room. She didn't see them go in. The man placed Lumerso's arm over his back and dragged him into the bedroom, throwing him on the bed. He stripped him. Placed him on his back. Lumerso's penis was the only thing still awake. The man savored it in every way, he licked it, used it to penetrate his own ass without a condom. He enjoyed Lumerso's dick until he came. Then the man left without leaving him a single peso.

Two hours later Lumerso woke up. His headache was better. His body ached. He felt a need to go to the bathroom. Noticed that the man had penetrated him, bitten his neck and back, on the mirror he contemplated the four bruises on the back of his neck.

Fuck him! I can't believe I didn't wake up! he thought

A heavy banging on the door startled him.

"It's been more than three hours," yelled a very unfriendly man.

Lumerso replied that he was getting ready to leave. He remembered he had no money. It was past six in the morning.

He walked for almost forty minutes until he made it to Romita. Julieta was already awake.

"We're not going anywhere?" she asked.

"I don't have a single peso on me," Lumerso answered as he sat on the couch.

He slept until midnight, when Julieta woke him, so he'd go to bed. Lumerso watched her with his owl-like eyes. Then he hugged her, giving her a long kiss on the cheek. Julieta didn't respond.

Chapter V

Jalisco, 2015

Gabriel became another of the many love interests of Lumerso. He was tall, had salt and pepper hair, was married and had five children. Lumerso had remained a handsome young man despite the late nights, the alcohol and the destructive lifestyle. Thanks to swimming he'd gotten a great looking back, phenomenal six pack abs, thick legs, and round buttocks. The face was the least important because what he had between his legs compensated his less than well-shaped nose and the scared eyes that characterized him. His smile would melt anyone. They adored him at the stores, restaurants, clubs, or any other place where he would show off his pearly whites. Though it might seem otherwise, deep down he was as humble as his mother and as noble as his father.

Gabriel was the owner of one of the largest textile businesses in the country, as well as one of most productive livestock ranches in the state of Jalisco. Lumerso had the opportunity to visit it on several occasions. To keep him close, Gabriel had introduced him to his family as a candidate for one of the vacant posts in the company. Laura, his wife, observed their every movement. She didn't buy Gabriel's story. Laura used Paco, her youngest son, to find out what went on under the table. She wanted to know if they were playing footsie or touching each other indecently. Paquito never saw a thing. Laura was fed up with the gayish actions of her husband as well as him constantly making her look like an idiot.

Gabriel knew that she spied on him, and thus played his cards right. He was careful of every movement he and Lumerso made. In private Laura would scream at him and asked him how dare he parade his lovers in her home and in front of their children. Gabriel never replied. The silence angered Laura even more. It was a marriage controlled by Gabriel's parents; even having five children was their idea. That Sunday, after the meal ended, they all gathered to watch a movie in the playroom. The kids crowded together on the floor. Gabriel took the armchair and Laura the couch along with Lumerso. About ten minutes after the movie started Gabriel said that something didn't agree with him and he should better go rest for a while. Half an hour later Lumerso mentioned that he'd already seen the movie and would be going for a walk. He slipped quietly out the backdoor. A small, quiet dog walked alongside Lumerso. The kids and Laura were left alone watching the movie. Laura wanted to go see how her husband was doing. Just before she got to the bedroom, she heard Gabriel's moans, they were the same he'd make when they were together. She tried to open the door, but it was locked. Enraged, Laura knocked several times until Gabriel opened. As she entered, the wind shook the curtains. She saw Lumerso disappearing into the garden after jumping out of the window. This time the dog barked.

"Son of a fucking bitch!" Laura yelled from the window.

Gabriel didn't answer. He finished getting dressed. He slipped out through the same window as Lumerso. Laura looked at that bed with all the hate in the world. She was fed up with her fake marriage. How could she have married someone she never loved? The only revenge was destroying him and taking everything from him in the divorce. A week later they started the paperwork.

Gabriel found Lumerso hiding behind the gate to the ranch. The ranch hand was beginning to herd the livestock and as he moved past them, he didn't even try to conceal the mocking expression on his face. Gabriel handed a shirt to Lumerso as well as a pair of five hundred pesos bills. He asked him to wait for him, that he'd go get the Jeep, so he could take the eight o'clock bus. Deep down Lumerso was annoyed by everything about Gabriel; especially how authoritarian he was. He hated that he treated him like Laura. He said no. Lumerso had no shoes either. Gabriel's boots were big, but he put them on anyway. He began walking. A stone road would take him to the town.

"See you next Friday," Gabriel said, trying to kiss him.

Lumerso avoided him. He knew it was the last time he'd see him. He kept walking with the shirt in his hand. The short relationship with Gabriel wasn't bad; yet his personal life was a source of conflict. He couldn't solve his troubles either. He thought about how much they'd done together; but having to listen to Gabriel talk about his children one more time was enough for Lumerso to go. Gabriel wanted to see his smile one more time. Lumerso didn't look back. He placed the shirt over his shoulder. Took him half an hour to walk the two kilometers of road to the station. The bus left at eight that night.

Chapter VI

Popocatepetl, 2003

In every relationship he had, Lumerso thought he saw the love of his life. He gave himself completely to every man. They all made the most of that kindness, squeezing out every drop of love he had to give. Each lover was a unique experience, a genuine love to him. With this, the list of clients multiplied; and yet, he lived confused and lost, not knowing his own identity. He couldn't figure out why hadn't he been able to do something else with his life. The sex had become his medicine, his food, his hobby, his everyday job. He couldn't remember how it was that he began to live like that. Couldn't pinpoint if it was after the death of his father, or the departure of his best friend, Edgar; or perhaps it was that time he made the first trip with the Boy Scouts. He would've been barely thirteen years old and hadn't yet become a man, as his father used to say.

One day, Lumerso and his father went to the market to stock up on food for a field trip with the scouts that would take place at the end of the school year. Antonio, the team captain, was a blonde from Los Cabos, with light-colored eyes and bleached hair. He wore ripped denim jeans. During their time together Lumerso would gaze with tremendous curiosity at the bulge peeking through one of the holes by the zipper. Antonio knew it and did nothing to hide the way he touched his own cock.

After they were done with the shopping, Lumerso had a cooler full of ground beef, rice, sausages, coffee, cheese and spaghetti. Ignacio, his father, took him to Antonio's place. He wanted to leave the cooler there, so they didn't have to carry it the next day. The young man who opened the door and received the supplies told them that Antonio was out jogging.

At half past five in the morning Antonio arrived. Lumerso ran, finished packing his bag and climbed on the back of the truck. A cold wind caressed his face. A boy he didn't know sat beside Antonio. Lumerso watched them both through the glass. Antonio would talk to him while touching his head every so often. Lumerso didn't know what he was feeling, but it bothered him.

Upon arriving at the parking lot where they would meet with the other guys Lumerso began to feel like he was sick. He told Antonio he wasn't going, and to take him back home. In response, Antonio took him behind the vehicle and touched his cheek, begging him to stay and saying that he had a surprise for him. Then he took his hand and intertwined his fingers with his own. Lumerso felt that his heart was in his throat; he never thought Antonio would be touching him in such a provocative way. Lumerso felt as if all the blood in his body was rushing to his head. Antonio took the chance to touch his lower lip, which Lumerso began biting nervously. He kissed him. Having worked with children for so many years gave him a certainty in knowing when one was gay. He was never wrong. Antonio had a well-built body and a graceful personality. He had been in the delegation in charge of the juvenile group of Boy Scouts for several years. In all that time none of the boy scouts ever complained about him; neither did any rumors reach their parents' ears.

"Coming then?" Antonio asked.

Lumerso agreed that he would.

When they arrived, they parked and walked close to the base of the Popocatepetl, where they'd camp for a couple of days. The cooler was heavy. It was difficult for Lumerso to have to drag it. He was always the last one to get anywhere. Antonio, who was at the front of the line, went back for him. He took the cooler and lifted it onto his shoulder. Lumerso smiled. The same boy who had sat beside Antonio looked at him with jealousy.

Upon arrival, they unpacked their bags and assembled the tents. Each scout was responsible for a chore. Lumerso was the one who had to cook the spaghetti with the ground beef he brought. He put everything in a pot with cold water and placed it over the fire. Seeing what was happening, Antonio ran to the rescue once again, showing Lumerso how to cook correctly.

Before the sunset they lit other bonfires. The group of eight distributed themselves among four tents. Antonio didn't want to share with anyone else; he told Lumerso they'd sleep together to protect him from the boys who were bothering him. Lumerso nodded and moved his sleeping bag to Antonio's tent. The dark sky that night was illuminated by the stars and a fading moon. That night they drank hot cocoa, played at being drunk men and told scary stories. They said goodnight a little after nine. Antonio's tent was in the middle. The stars provided a wonderful spectacle of lights. The night was freezing. Some insects chirped. The moon hid behind the volcano, the campfire stopped shining fiercely. Antonio went for more firewood, then stayed out for a while enjoying some coffee. The cold was increasing, it was almost inhuman to remain there. He placed the rest of the firewood on the bonfires before running into the tent. Lumerso was sleeping peacefully. His cheeks were pink and there was a slight smile on his face. The cold didn't bother him. He was wearing all his clothes, plus two winter jackets, aside from the two woolen hats his Grandma Victoria gave him as a gift.

Antonio touched his cheeks and got closer to him. Asked if he was alive. Lumerso heard him but didn't answer. Then he felt the light. The lantern was illuminating Antonio's face, his Antonio. He waited for him to kiss him like he had that morning, but Antonio didn't look for his trembling lips. Upset, he told him to go back to his dreams, that tomorrow was going to be a day with many activities. Confused, Lumerso turned his face away. A few seconds later Antonio said he was freezing, that they should sleep in the same bag.

Lumerso accepted. Antonio embraced Lumerso's little body until they both fell asleep.

The next morning no one wanted to get up. The temperature, despite being the middle of summer, had gone down below zero; the cold was like that of the Russian tundra. Lumerso was sleeping too. Antonio kissed him in the lips, slowly slipping his tongue inside. Lumerso felt sick. He thought of his bad breath, and how terrible Antonio tasted. Antonio pulled off Lumerso's layers of clothing, quickly getting to his buttocks. Then licked him like a cat until he got to Lumerso's penis. Lumerso felt a wet, warm mouth for the first time on his dick. It was as if some incredible pleasure had taken over him. He couldn't believe that so much pleasure could exist. He didn't want him to stop, so Antonio continued until a load of crystalline semen shot from Lumerso. He kissed him again. This time Lumerso felt a taste he didn't dislike.

"Tonight, we'll do something else," Antonio told him.

Midmorning, after breakfast, they went looking for volcanic rocks, local insects and did some exploration going as far as two hundred meters around. Antonio and Lumerso walked towards one of the streams by the volcano. A creek of crystalline water was covered with pine needles. Green ferns surrounded the spring. They settled under the trees, contemplating the Popocatepetl. Water kept slowly moving downstream.

"Are we boyfriends now?" Lumerso asked with a voice starting to change with age.

Antonio understood this wasn't his only question. He changed topic, challenging him to go into the water.

"Are you crazy, it must be freezing," Lumerso replied.

Antonio began to disrobe. Lumerso didn't really see exactly when he got into the water. Seconds later, Lumerso followed. They were both freezing. Antonio hugged the delicate body of Lumerso, embracing him and then kissing him with passion.

"What happens between you and I, no one must know," Antonio finally said, shivering from the cold.

His teeth were chattering. A strong wind forced them out of the water. Antonio carried Lumerso in his arms. It was time to eat. Everyone stared at the two who were wet as mops as they arrived back at the campsite. Antonio lit the fire and improvised a meal. That night, one of the boys fell sick with a terrible toothache and they had to abandon the camp. Lumerso's place was the last stop Antonio made as he dropped the members of the troop off.

"What happened cannot happen again," Antonio stressed.

A glimpse of sadness ruined Lumerso's new memories. He got out of the truck leaving the door open.

"The door!" Antonio yelled angrily.

Lumerso kept walking without looking back. Antonio didn't see him again until three months later, when he went to say goodbye before returning to Los Cabos. Lumerso seemed to have grown. He was wearing a uniform with khaki pants and a white shirt. He had a few pimples on his face, but that didn't change him. Lumerso couldn't believe that he was about to cross the whole country in that old heap. Not even a single box more would fit in the truck.

"I've told you that I'm getting on the ferry departing from Mazatlan," Antonio reminded Lumerso.

Lumerso had in his hands a box with two seashells. He bought them with Grandma Victoria at the Lagunilla market. Antonio took the gift and placed it in the glove compartment. They looked at each other for a long while without saying a word. Antonio touched his arm subtly with his little finger.

"I have to go," Lumerso declared.

"Me too," Antonio answered.

The gray truck rode until taking a left on Mexico Avenue, to then disappear by the Insurgentes Avenue. Antonio hoped that Lumerso wouldn't tell anyone.

Chapter VII

Escandon Neighborhood, 2019

Lumerso is lounging on an old chair near a closet. A strong smell of gas permeates the place. On the TV an insipid porno movie plays in the background. Some aggressive footsteps pound on the metal staircase. The night is over. Wilfredo, the cleaner, sweeps the rooms with lack of enthusiasm while listening to *banda* music on a portable radio. Wilfredo hates his job; picking up condoms filled with shit every day isn't the best job in the world. The loudmouth woman that sells mattresses hasn't been by yet, but he thought he heard the man who sells *tamales*. Grandma Victoria hated them! That was one of the worst things in Mexico City. Aside from the extreme environmental pollution, the crime, drug traffickers, and blasting of the horns wherever you went, now they allowed anyone to use a fucking loudspeaker and create even more noise pollution. Lumerso isn't as upset by it as before. Now it allows him to identify the hours of the day. Sometimes he counts them walking by five or six times a day; others, as far as ten. He imagined the mattress-seller as an obese girl, with cinnamon skin, yelling into a microphone. Nowadays she'd be a married woman, with four children, locked in her house, cooking, and doing housework. He pictures the *tamales* vendor as a restless boy, probably a daring personality, perhaps even mischievous. A person who looked for immediate fame and found it. He wonders why he couldn't find that notoriety, that love, everything he longed for in life.

Life had been unfair to him; the opportunities never showed up; and if they did, he couldn't see them. He's still there, in the same place, looking at social inequality and lewd love. It's perhaps divine punishment; seeing every day what he once desired. Lumerso wants to cry. He feels sorrow, pain, hopelessness. Doesn't know where it hurts or where the thoughts come from, the memories. He banishes the tears. Remembers his grandmother's words, his mother's, his father's. He misses the comfort of his house in Condesa, his bed, even his sister's tantrums. He cannot change anything anymore; he can only remember. He thinks about what a relationship with Edgar would've been like. Loves, so many loves to whom he gave his body... for what? To end up here, in a call house, with men desperate to get some nice ass or a tremendous cock. Sex was what now caused him the most revulsion.

Through the window he sees a leaf trying to get inside. The leaf ends up trapped. He pushes it so it won't get in. Talks to it. He himself doesn't know what he says. It insists on going in. He thinks about the languages, the etiquette and the history lessons his Grandma Victoria tried to teach him, everything he never cared about. The leaf gives up and falls to the floor. It'll stay there for a long time. Wilfredo never picks them up, they're not condoms. Lumerso would like to pick it up. Protect it from that hardship. Maybe outside it might have a better life! Sunlight pierces through the terrace. He hears a racket of cars. He knows he cannot go out there. He takes in some air, closes his eyes. He senses someone coming. They're starting to arrive.

A guy in denim and a striped button-up shirt comes in. He unbuttons the first couple of buttons of the shirt. A chain with a silver cross hanging from his neck sways on his chest. He opens his fly. Steps into the darkness. Lumerso waits until he sees the man with the mustache whip in hand; he might be drunk or high. He finds it odd to see him at the time of the *tamales*. He observes him until Wilfredo speaks to him:

"We're closed between ten and eleven for cleaning."

The man with the mustache walks towards the door, though not before picking up a couple of condoms and throwing them at Wilfredo's face.

"And these?" the man says with no emotion.

Mustache climbs the stairs until he disappears. The man in the striped shirt comes out scared and follows him.

"Fucking jackass, he left unfulfilled," Wilfredo mocks.

The cleaner is right. The place usually closes to handle daily cleaning. The owner hired straight, elderly people for that task; that way they wouldn't hook up with the clients during the day. Most died already. Wilfredo was the only one left from the group. He was in charge of picking up the underwear left on the floor, condoms, belts, shirts, cigarette packs, cellphones or any other object lost in the midst of passion. Their owners never returned for them. Who would want to go back for a pair of pink silk panties? Sometimes he found wallets with all their personal information. Wilfredo collects them and keeps the money. He had even thought about the possibility of blackmailing one of them. He would go as far as practicing out loud what he could tell them, but in the end, he'd always changed his mind. Once he went to the grocery store with one of the credit cards to buy a coffee, some cookies, and a cigarette pack. The cashier saw his scared face. Asked him for an ID. Wilfredo ran away, spilling the coffee all the way back to work. After that, he never wanted to do it again. *It's better to be a poor slob, than a schmuck with money,* he told himself.

Lumerso's family had lived their whole lives in the Condesa neighborhood. In one of the streets adjacent to the Mexico Park. Ignacio, his father, worked as an accountant in an outsourcing company; his mother, Josefina, was a dedicated housewife. She studied nursing but her nervous condition stopped her from practicing. Regardless, on the topic of their family's finances life smiled at them from the start. Lumerso had an older sister that went to high-school and part of her college in Swiss schools. He chose to stay in the country. He was a boy who liked the city, the baguettes in the San Juan market and the capital's messy scene. His father always reminded his children that they had exactly the same opportunities as others and that none of them were the favorite, and none of them should feel better than others.

Grandma Victoria, Josefina's mother, lived with them since her return from Australia. She kept Lumerso's secrets. They would chat until late at night. She knew about his latest love affairs. She would advise him, tell him that there were so many other important things to focus on. She told him about civilizations that had disappeared from humanity, just as would happen with our own, because everything ends so it can be reborn. Lumerso wouldn't listen, he was a dreamer who believed in that eternal love that he saw in his grandmothers' soap operas.

Grandma Victoria married a French diplomat and traveled through the five continents. Or so she said. She spoke four languages and claimed she knew the world like the back of her hand. After having lived in Canberra for more than two decades, she returned to Mexico, since she wanted to die where she'd been born. François, her husband, died of a heart attack. She refused to end her life in a foreign retirement home. She returned to Mexico and moved in with the De la Torre family. Three years later, she died due to lung illness and with two pesos to her name. Lumerso wondered if everything his grandma said was true; the travels, the dinners, and the diplomat husband. There were no photographs of anything to back her stories. Only her words.

After the death of Grandma Victoria, Lumerso isolated himself. He didn't want to spend time with his parents anymore and never talked about his private life with anyone other than his diary. Ignacio, like Josefina, suspected that his son was attracted to boys. His whole childhood he threw tantrums in the toy stores whenever he didn't get the same doll as his sister Julieta. Josefina tried to comfort him but couldn't find the adequate words for him to understand her. As children, Julieta would gift him her dolls. He enjoyed playing with Ken and Barbie as the perfect couple. On Three Kings Day, when Lumerso had just turned seven, his father bought him a soccer ball and a game with toy cars; he also got Julieta a doll house with all the accessories. Lumerso took the toy cars and the ball and kicked them like a maniac in the backyard. He cried and screamed until his father locked him up in his bedroom for the rest of the day. Once he got out, Lumerso spoke like a grown-up:

"There's no need for you to buy me more toys, if they're not the ones I want."

His father thought that what Lumerso said was fair and sensible. That was the last year he got a gift on Three Kings Day.

Chapter VIII

Romita, 2010

The body of Ignacio de la Torre lay in his coffin. The kind smile and laid-back personality he was known for were gone. Lumerso stared at him for a long while without crying. Julieta observed Lumerso from the other end of Ignacio's coffin. Josefina exhibited an almost unnatural calmness, courtesy of a couple of valiums. Lumerso couldn't comprehend how a person could die like Ignacio did, without warning. He thought it was very selfish of Ignacio. More importantly, what was he going to live on, since he was still a long way from finishing his degree. No one in the family was prepared for Ignacio's untimely departure.

Lumerso couldn't stand the room that was closing in around him, the nauseating smell of the flowers and the whispering of people whose names he couldn't remember. The weighing sense that his life had changed. Lumerso stepped out seeking some air. He was surprised to meet Edgar, smoking a cigarette. Edgar, more handsome than ever. He was wearing a pair of checkered trousers, a white button-up, and a black, skinny tie. Edgar hugged him for a long while.

"I'm very, truly, sorry, my friend," Edgar said.

Edgar was still waiting for an answer, when Lumerso wiggled out of his arms, kept walking until he found a bathroom and locked himself in. Edgar waited for twenty minutes before knocking. Lumerso didn't answer. Edgar kept people away when they came looking for a bathroom, told them there was another on the second floor. A half an hour later, Lumerso opened the door, pulled Edgar in, and locked the door from the inside. Lumerso kissed him passionately, telling him how much he loved him, how much he'd missed him.

Lumerso always said Edgar was the only person who understood him. The two shared everything during their childhood; lunches, bike rides, homework, measuring penises to see whose was still growing. But now? Edgar was engaged. He had proposed to a bland *gringo*, John, he met in Washington, D.C. Edgar planned to return to Mexico to work in his father's pharmaceutical company. He was on his way there when he learned of Ignacio's death. He regretted leaving without saying goodbye. But he hadn't wanted everyone to find out that, just like Lumerso, he too, was gay. Edgar had hated Lumeroso for a long time. He blamed Lumerso for his childhood identity crisis. Yet, he could never stop thinking about Lumeroso.

Lumerso kept kissing Edgar as his white shirt and checkered trousers fell to the floor. Lumerso took some soap, slathered it on Edgar's anus and without a pause, penetrated him. Edgar wanted to scream, whether in pleasure or pain he didn't know, but Lumerso clapped his hand over Edgar's mouth. Both quietly moaned. Lumerso gently mussed Edgar's hair, then roughly yanked him until he had half Edgar's body splayed out over the sink. Lumerso opened Edgar's legs. Took pleasure from him as he always dreamed of while he masturbated Edgar's massive erection. After just a few minutes both ejaculated simultaneously. Edgar suddenly couldn't comprehend what had just happened. He had imagined that moment, but not the way it took place. Edgar threw on his clothes and fled, leaving Lumerso sitting on the toilet seat.

When the door closed, Lumerso began to cry. His father had died. He was suffocating with pain. He hysterically screamed Edgar's name. But Edgar was already at the viaduct light, heading as far and as quickly away as he could. As people rushed toward the bathroom, Lumerso fainted hitting himself on the stall wall as he fell on the floor.

Julieta studied Lumerso from her chair at the foot of his bed. She realized that the hospital bed was smaller than Ignacio's coffin. Lumerso's complexion was jaundiced. Tubes supplied him with air to breathe. Lumerso had been unconscious for the six days since his breakdown in the bathroom of the funeral parlor and Ignacio's burial. Julieta was wearing the same black dress she wore to the funeral. Her eyes were red, she had dark circles around them, and she looked haggard. Make-up was a distant memory. Outside of the window a couple of sparrows could be heard singing. It was the last days of spring. A foggy city awaited her on the streets. Julieta had but one thought: she couldn't lose her brother. She had lost everything else or was about to. After the funeral she learned Ignacio had mortgaged the house from Condesa, which they now had lost. Julieta managed to hold on to the apartment in Romita that her father bought for her after her return from Switzerland, though it was practically unlivable since it was still not furnished. Disgrace weighed heavily upon her. She arranged Lumerso's pillow and kissed him on the forehead. Julieta was already expecting the worst. A voice surprised her.

"I missed the funeral... didn't I?" Lumerso said in a broken voice.

Julieta kissed him again. For the first time in six days she felt a glimmer of happiness.

Two months later they were all in the apartment in Romita. Ignacio's accumulated bills covered the kitchen table. Julieta was working in the post of secretary in the public sector. Their mother spent her days lost in a tranquilizer-induced world of distant thoughts and incoherent memories. Lumerso, in Julieta's room, refused to look at his mother. He spent his days on his cellphone looking for temporary jobs. He finally found one in the bus station, getting passengers on the buses at the terminal. The pursue of his degree was placed on hold. He didn't have a clue regarding what he'd do next with his life. His father's death turned his entire family's lives upside down. The bastard died without leaving them a single peso. Now the story of their lives was a starting a new chapter they didn't know how it would end.

After having worked for two weeks helping people on and off the buses, Lumerso noticed a man in a suit and tie moving his tongue suggestively in circles around his mouth. Lumerso watched him for several days without saying a word to him. Early one Sunday morning, Lumerso found the man sitting alone at the back of an empty bus. As Lumerso approached him, the man spread his legs and showed Lumerso his enormous penis straining against the fabric of his white pants. Lumerso felt everything except attraction.

"What the fuck's wrong with you?" Lumerso yelled angrily.

The man squeezed his cock suggestively one more time and invited him to go out after work. Lumerso didn't understand why he accepted. They went to a place by the station for *tacos*. He said his name was Genaro and told him there were better ways for a handsome, indeed magnificent, young man like Lumerso to make a living. Intrigued, Lumerso asked how. Genaro told Lumerso he liked darker young guys like him very much and suggested they go to a hotel on the Alvaro Obregon Avenue. Genaro offered Lumerso five hundred pesos if he played the role of passive. Lumerso hesitated since Genaro seemed to have an elephant trunk between his legs. Lumerso then surprised himself and countered with an offer of six hundred. Genaro accepted on the spot and the deal was sealed.

The hotel was filthy and stunk of old beer and older sex. The comforters were full of cigarette burns, and the walls were covered in various unidentifiable bodily fluids. A half curtain covered part of a cell-like window. There were two mirrors, the bigger one was above them, and the other one at one side of the bed. The window over the bed looked into a wall in the garden. Lumerso took a little of the water in the pitcher on a nightstand.

"Can't guarantee it's clean," Genaro said.

Lumerso wasn't sure what he was talking about and took the water. Genaro placed the money on top of the TV, where a porno movie had just started, then went into the bathroom. He spied on Lumerso through the mirror. Lumerso was about to take the money and run, but at that moment Genaro came out with the biggest erection Lumerso had seen in his life.

"For six hundred pesos you're eating all of this, fucker," Genaro said proudly.

Lumerso took off his clothes, his eyes locked on Genaro's monster penis. Lumerso suddenly felt hatred towards his father and a horrible anger at his own life rising from deep inside him. After, he felt so powerless that he threw himself face down on the mattress. As if Lumerso were a child, Genaro gently rubbed lube in his rectum, going in and out with his finger until Lumerso's ass hole was lubricated. Then, he roughly flipped him over, lifted his legs and slowly penetrated him.

"Aren't you going to wear a condom?" Lumerso gasped.

"Not today," Genaro replied.

Lumerso went limp while Genaro's animal instincts took over: he fucked him so hard Lumerso swore Genaro was punching his organs. When Genaro finally ejaculated inside him, Lumerso lay on the bed exhausted and aching. He didn't know what the hell he had just been through: a hook up, prostitution, or a rape.

As if reading his thoughts Genaro said, "The more you're willing to do and the more people you're willing to do it with, the more money I will give you."

Genaro then asked Lumerso for his cellphone number and rushed out.

Now he really was a *putito*, *Thanks dad*, thought Lumerso with sarcasm. He'd just gotten more money than he made in a week. He returned home with a couple of liters of milk, a kilo of *tortillas* and a roasted chicken. His mother was still seated in the same position where he left her that morning. Watching the TV, which was turned off, reacting to a show that only she could see. Julieta didn't say a word about Lumerso's purchases. They all sat on the couch to eat. No one spoke. Lumerso kept thinking about the sharp pain he could still feel and Genaro's depraved face as he ejaculated into him.

Chapter IX

Condesa Neighborhood, 2004

"May 24th, 2004

Forgive me that I had nothing to write to you until now, but I want to tell you that I'm in love. I don't dare write his name, as excited as I am, but it's someone that comes to my place every Sunday for lunch and stays the afternoon to watch the game with dad. My father always calls me into the TV room asking me to bring them this or that; and when he sees me, he also asks me for something. You know who he is, right? Yeah, it's Teran, dad's friend. When they get excited watching the game, they tap each other. I feel a bit jealous. Dad punches him lightly on the shoulder and Teran pats him on the back. They ask me to watch the game with them. I get hooked on the bodies of the football players, watching the movement of their legs and the waggling

*of their dicks. Then I find any excuse to leave. I believe
that if dad knew what I'm thinking he'd give me a good
slap in the neck. Teran reminds me very much of
Antonio, but that one for sure doesn't want me anymore.
I imagine he must even have some other boyfriend and
has forgotten all about me by now. I don't care at all
because I've forgotten him too. You tell me what I must
do, I don't know if I should write a note to invite him to
go with me and my dog Oliver to the park. I know he
must be in love with me too. I love him like crazy,
though I love Edgar too. I can have many boyfriends,
right?*

    *Imagine if he took me to Toluca where it's very,
very cold and we had to sleep tightly together both of
us, it'd be like a dream. Today he was wearing some
blue pants, those that have some white stripes on the
sides. He had a white t-shirt on and a brown jacket.
They always sit together on the couch in the TV room.
He opens his big legs and first he has a glass of water;
but later, with the excitement of the game, they have
some beers together. Yesterday I was unplugging my
new X-Box and he asked me if I needed help. I almost
answered yes but then dad stared at me and I told him
no thank you. My heart was bursting out my chest.
Once here in my room I noticed I'd forgotten the cable
and had to go back. This time he unplugged it and
placed it on my hands. I felt his big hands grazing mine.
I know he did it on purpose because I don't think
anyone else touches me that way. I went back to my
room and left the X-Box on mute so that I could hear
when the game ended. When I heard nothing, I went
down to see what had happened. The famous Chivas
had lost, and their faces looked like it was a tragedy.*

Dad ordered me to take the empty bottles and I saw how Teran was putting on his jacket. I offered him a hand and told him I was very sorry they'd lost. He pulled me by the arm and hugged me. You see, can you tell, he's in love with me too. Dad stared at him strangely, but didn't say a thing. I ran off and locked myself here in my room. I didn't want to tell you anything, but later I told myself that it was better to write it all down; that way, I won't forget."

"February 14th, 2005

Dear diary,

Nothing ever happens in my life. Since Chivas lost, Teran no longer comes to the house to see the games. Once, I saw him at the grocery store with his wife. She's very pretty. I didn't know he was married. Cannot understand either why if he was married, he came to the house alone. Today is the Day of the Lovers, of Saint Valentine, or Day of the Friends. I don't know anymore. The whole world walks around with hearts, stuffed toys, chocolates, and I don't know what other nonsensical stuff. I'd like to fall in love again.

Grandma Victoria is crazy. She always says I have to focus on other things and never on love. I think that maybe she had a bad experience and doesn't feel the way I do. I bought some boxes of chocolates and gave one to everyone, even to Jimena, our maid. That way they can tell I have love for them. Teran, Antonio, and Edgar. You see that in my life nothing happens, that since Edgar left, I barely even use the bike. Besides, mom is always yelling at me not to forget the helmet. It weighs a lot and it is useless. Every time I fall, I always hit my knees and never the head, never the head!

Edgar's mom says he went to Washington, D.C. I don't believe her; I think he's hidden away in some school around Satelite. You know, I miss him a ton, but never mind, that's how love is. Oliver is getting more and more sick. The veterinarian says it'll be a short time before he dies, but I, even with all of that, still take him to the park; even though he doesn't walk like before anymore. I've already got experience in this and when I am an older man, I'm going to give classes on what love is and what it's for. I can hear them calling me for dinner, so I'll leave you for now, but then I'll come tell you about all I did today, on Saint Valentine's, though you're my one and only Valentine."

"*February 15th, 2005*

I knew this was going to happen. I didn't receive any gifts for Saint Valentine's. Though I don't care, I'm only telling you. We all sat at the table and my father brought my mom some flowers. They were cool, but she didn't give them much importance. Mom placed them on the console table. I see my mother getting weirder and weirder. She only speaks once in a blue moon... maybe she's ill or something? Jimena does whatever she wants now. Mom no longer asks her what's she's cooking that day or tells her to clean the windows. Jimena doesn't ask either. She spends all day in the kitchen doing I-don't-know-what. Yesterday I was looking for my t-shirt for my Physical Education class.

I found it in the drier with a bunch of clothes she hadn't yet folded. They're both very strange… or maybe all women are like that.

Yesterday, since I didn't have any Valentines, I closed my eyes while I ate the stew to imagine my Phys Ed professor. Sometimes I think he knows I'm gay. He doesn't order me to exercise like the others, or to run. I insist that I must do the same as everyone else. On Monday we did some laps around the court and he wouldn't look at anyone else but me. Then he asked me if I wanted a glass of water. He didn't offer one to anyone else. Only to me. Maybe he likes me. I think he's a very cool guy, but I wouldn't like him to be my boyfriend. I think physical attraction is one thing, but the attraction one feels for a special person is something else. What do you think? I'm leaving you now. I leave you to think about it. I need to practice for the Biology presentation about DNA tests to find the true guilty parties of crimes of the past. That'll be all for now. Bye!!!"

Chapter X

Escandon Neighborhood, 2019

A strong storm hits the downtown area of the city. The rainwater goes down through the staircases, flooding the floors. Harsh winds blow everything they find in their path. The water drags along a line of condoms, toilet paper and trash. A chair falls from the terrace to end up in the basement. The men don't come out. Some hide like hens. Spurts of water form puddles everywhere. Lumerso hides under one of the sinks. In the TV room several people smoke pot. Lumerso thinks that maybe hitting some of that would do him good. It's nighttime. The storm's getting worse. Lightning followed by thunder light up the sky. A tree falls on a parallel street. A man stumbles as he escorts a young guy to the room with the bunk beds. He pulls out a couple of bills and hands them over. Others are waiting for them. The excitement grows.

The first rains of May were just beginning to fall, Lumerso lost the journal. It had been raining for three days. He didn't care. He took the raincoat, the schoolbag and left for class. The English Teacher had been absent. The Chemistry teacher was always there. That day there were few students. Lumerso, as usual, sat in the back. He wasn't in the mood for chatting or making stupid questions. He wanted to write in the journal, searched for it desperately, but couldn't find it. The noise disrupted the class.

"Something we could help you with?" Mr. Gutierrez, the teacher, asked as he noticed the ruckus.

Lumerso left the class in a state of shock. He stumbled over a couple of tables on his way out. The wind slammed shut the classroom door. He ran until he made it to where he'd left his bicycle. It would take him fifteen minutes to get home. The hard-falling rain soaked him and made it very hard to see ahead. A soda truck almost ran him over. Lumerso pedaled for ten minutes until he made it to the gate of his house. He ran to his room and began looking everywhere for his journal. He couldn't find it. Jimena asked what he was looking for. Lumerso didn't answer. He searched under the mattress, in the nightstand's drawers, the desk. He went down the stairs, threw cushions all over the place, searched in the TV room, underneath the furniture, until finally Jimena asked again:

"Are you looking for the green notebook?"

Lumerso felt like his heart suddenly stopped beating. He approached Jimena and took her by the shoulders, yelling at her to give it back to him. Jimena told him his parents had it while they argued during breakfast. That they talked about Mr. Teran and the relationship he had with him. A thought about slapping her, like in the soap operas, crossed Lumerso's mind. It would be a great punishment for gossiping. Surely that was how they knew everyone's lives, by listening behind the doors.

"Mom, where is she?" Lumerso asked, he was irate.

Jimena replied that she'd gone out to get her hair done, but she was sure to be back soon. He called her mother's cellphone several times but got no answer. Then he went up to his room and stayed there for the rest of the day. Mr. Gutierrez called to know if everything was alright with Lumerso. Jimena told him all the details about the so-called missing notebook.

Lumerso didn't go down to eat all day. Neither of his parents went up to talk to him. The next day he got up as if nothing had changed and came downstairs for breakfast. His father was about to leave, and his mother was having a cup of coffee.

"We'll talk tonight," Ignacio announced.

Lumerso shrugged but said nothing. His mother greeted him with the usual kiss.

The annoying drizzle kept getting everything wet. Lumerso didn't take the bike, he decided to walk. Same as the night before, he was trying to remember what he'd written in the journal. He thought again about Antonio, about Teran, about Edgar, about the Phys Ed teacher and all the stupid stories written inside it. He regretted putting his life into words. It made no sense to think that someone else might be interested in the experiences or anecdotes that he himself found boring. He couldn't blame Jimena for stealing it either;

surely, he must have forgotten it on the kitchen table. He didn't want to be himself, he wanted to change his motherboard and become someone else.

How could it be stolen? That was a violation of human rights! It wasn't great that his parents chose to disrespect him like that. He wanted to leave, to eliminate them from his life. Wanted to forget he was a member of the De la Torre family. Thought about phoning Julieta, but perhaps she too was an accomplice. They were all accomplices, even Jimena now knew everything about his private life. Surely over there, in the Buenos Aires neighborhood, they all now knew about the gay things he'd done.

Lumerso decided to skip class and spent the time at the swimming club. He swam backstroke for an hour and a half, until he felt his body so light that he thought about eating a cow. He approached the shower. On the other side of the showers was Arturo. Arturo was a boy who was training for the Pan-American Games. He was 1.90 meters tall, had the best athletic body Lumerso had ever seen. Sometimes he'd saw him in the pool, but today was his lucky day. Arturo was in the shower, naked and beautiful as he always imagined him. Lumerso observed him for several minutes until his penis changed in size. He took the soap and lathered it all over his body. His dick was covered in foam. Arturo excited him. Lumerso bent several times, showing him his buttocks. He stroked the muscles of his pectorals. The foam ran quickly down the drains. Arturo grabbed his cock and began to masturbate. Lumerso forgot how tired he was. Arturo signaled for him to close the entry door. Lumerso shook his head, hesitating for a moment before he did as asked and then walked towards him.

At eleven in the morning the place was empty. If someone else arrived, it'd be a senior citizen who surely wouldn't be able to hear or see them since they were in the last two showers. They began to kiss until Lumerso wanted to penetrate him. Arturo didn't want it. They kept kissing. The water drenched them, forming a veil that covered them both. They masturbated their penises until managing to get their chests lathered with a creamy white layer. Arturo smiled, rinsed himself under the shower, kissed his lips and stepped out cautiously. Lumerso waited until Arturo finished getting dressed before stepping out of the shower. He wanted to take his time. Thought it was a pity he didn't have the journal on him, since that would have been a darn good entry.

Lumerso spent all day wandering between the Condesa and Roma Norte neighborhoods. He went to several coffee shops. Ate *tacos* at El Guero of Amsterdam Avenue. He went by the school twice and it wasn't until after seven that he returned home. His father was sitting in the living room, working on a new project. Josefina went down the stairs as soon as she heard Lumerso coming in. No one said a thing. An uncomfortable silence gagged all of them.

"You have a plate in the oven," his mother said hurriedly.

"I'm not hungry," Lumerso answered.

Lumerso tossed his schoolbag over the couch. His mother looked at him. Then she approached Ignacio and whispered to him that it might be good if he talked to him. Ignacio didn't know what to say. He wasn't an emotional man, and much less so after having read some of the entries in the journal.

"Are the stories you wrote true?" his father asked impulsively.

Lumerso looked at him with resentment.

"What do you think?" Lumerso asked cynically.

Ignacio looked at Josefina as if he were searching for an answer in her eyes. No one dared say anything else.

"That filth you wrote… I asked Jimena to burn it," Ignacio said.

That ended up hurting Lumerso more. He rushed to his bedroom while trying to deal with a ginormous knot in his throat. They both knew about their son's homosexuality but didn't know how to face it. They talked about sending him back to the therapist or sending him to live with Julieta out of the country. Ignacio blurted any and all of his ideas without pondering them. When he was nervous, he'd blabber so many things that he later couldn't take back. He made sure to say, one more time, that in his family there were no faggots, that surely that problem came from her side. Josefina thought about the foolish and selfish man she was married to. They kept arguing without reaching any agreement.

Lumerso took the books from his bag and tossed them on the trash. He then grabbed a pair of jeans, t-shirts, and underwear, and placed everything inside his bag. He broke his piggy bank. 696.51 pesos. The savings of almost half a year.

He'd just turned seventeen and hated the distrust he now felt towards his parents. He couldn't live in a house of spies, of privacy invaders. He was no longer interested on who or how they found his journal. He hated what they did with it, with his words, with his true self. Lumerso decided to wait until his parents went to sleep. He pressed his head behind the door. He could hear the whispers of his mother and the yelling of his father. He put music on for a while until he fell asleep. He didn't know when that happened.

"It's time, Lumerso," Jimena yelled from the other side of the door.

Lumerso heard her voice. He felt anger for having slept all night. He went to the bathroom down the hall, got his hair wet and put away some more things in his schoolbag. He took a glass of orange juice. Gave a kiss to his mother. Opened the door and went out. Seconds later he went back in. He asked:

"Where did my journal ended up, Jimena?"

She hesitated for a few minutes not knowing how to tell him, until she finally confessed to having burned it in the backyard like his father ordered. Lumerso's face changed. He thought of his words burning in the fire, burning forever, becoming ashes. He didn't want to cry. He kissed his mother, this time giving her a hug.

"See you Jimena," he said goodbye trying not to look vindictive to her.

He walked without direction, not knowing what his next stop might be. He wouldn't be going back to school. He had nothing to do there anymore. That was not his home any longer. He'd seek a new course, new friends, would meet new people, and others to fall in love with. That's how his new life began.

Chapter XI

Taxqueña Metro Station, 2007

Lumerso arrived at the Taxqueña Station. He didn't know where he'd go. He thought about Cuernavaca, Acapulco or Los Cabos. He could perhaps call one of the scouts and ask him how or where to find Antonio. He'd forgive him for leaving. The idea didn't convince him. Without thinking too much about it he offered a man twenty pesos for him to buy him a ticket to Cuernavaca. Didn't want to be questioned for being a minor. He'd never traveled alone. The man, whom he never let out of his sight, returned with the ticket.

When the bus began going down the Federal Highway, he finally started to leave Mexico City behind. A black cloud covered the skyscrapers of Reforma Avenue. Lumerso remembered his classmates. All had girlfriends but him. After Edgar left for the United States, he started seeing Claudia, but he couldn't pretend what wasn't true. He drew with his finger his face reflected on the windowpane. He traced tears on the cheeks. A fog was beginning to cover the highway. He didn't know when he fell asleep.

Since Edgar's departure, Lumerso hadn't been able to open up to anyone else. Everyone assumed he was gay; yet no one accepted that he might date boys. His journal was his only escape. He vented there, he told it everything. Oliver, his dog, became his only friend until cancer killed him. Life was unfair and selfish, snatching from him everything he loved. He began his journal before finishing elementary; lately his entries grew thinner every month. Sometimes he'd write every day; others, the diary would be forgotten inside some drawer for weeks. It was his journal that got full details about the first masturbation Lumerso had the day Edgar slept over at his place. Also, in its pages was the entire story regarding what happened in Chapultepec. He wrote of when Edgar and he looked at each other for the first time in their speedos for swimming class. He'd like to turn back time, be a child again, be able to do all that like before. He didn't want to grow anymore. Edgar left without saying a thing. How could he forgive him? He never wanted to accept that he loved him; for that, he decided to leave.

The voice of the driver woke him up. When he got off the bus Lumerso didn't have the slightest idea as to what to do or where to go. He wanted to think that the four hundred pesos in his pocket would last him for a week. He walked downtown until he reached a coffee shop. He ordered a chocolate milk and a sweet bread. He thought of how much he missed the computer. It occurred to him to ask the waitress if she knew of a job. The girl told him that the owner of the place was looking for someone to wallpaper some walls in her house.

"I have no experience," Lumerso replied.

The girl told him to never repeat those words. She explained to him where the house was, so he could go as soon as he finished breakfast.

Lumerso knocked on the door. A lady with an arrogant air interrogated him:

"What's the reason for your visit?"

"I came to put up your wallpaper," Lumerso said, his voice shaking.

The woman let him in and began describing in detail what he was to do. She told him about the glue and informed him that he was to work very carefully, as she hated for the wallpaper to wrinkle.

"Do you have experience?" she asked.

Lumerso began to work while answering that he'd done it many times at home and that he loved the wallpaper. The woman didn't look like she believed him, but she seemed to like him. Lumerso began to read the instructions on how to mix the glue.

When he finished placing the last sheet of the wallpaper, he heard a younger voice speaking to him:

"My mother is going to kill you."

Eugenio was an only child. He attended a private school in Mexico City, but the bus didn't wait for him again that morning.

"Why is she going to kill me...? It has no wrinkles, just like she asked," Lumerso replied a bit mad.

"It's just that it's inside out," Eugenio pointed making a face.

Lumerso went pale. He wanted to flee. Just as he was about to grab his bag, Eugenio told him he was joking, that he'd done good work.

"Are you always this annoying?" Lumerso asked.

"Clearly you don't know what a sense of humor is," Eugenio replied.

It was past four o'clock. Lumerso's stomach was beginning to complain already. He was hungry. Lumerso took the money Eugenio handed him and walked to the door.

"You don't have to leave... I missed the school bus for the third time this week. I'm kind of bored," Eugenio said slowly.

"I'm hungry, so I wanna eat!" Lumerso declared.

They went straight to the kitchen. Pulled out ham and Oaxaca cheese to prepare some *chapatas*. They had them with some sodas. Lumerso told him that he'd ran away from his home and was never going back. He went on to tell him about the journal, what a bad thing they did to him by stealing it, but the worst part was that they burnt it. Eugenio wasn't good at talking, but he was entertained by listening to others. They finished eating and then went on to play with the XBOX. Eugenio asked him to pick up everything before his mom arrived. Between the two of them they put away the ladder and the floorcloth in a storage space in the backyard. Lumerso remembered he didn't have a place to stay. He wanted to ask, but the shame won.

"You can stay here!" Eugenio said as if he were reading his mind. Lumerso smiled. They played until past ten at night.

The next day Lumerso got up without making a noise. He wanted to leave a note but couldn't find where to write. He walked down Matamoros Avenue. He felt frustration at not knowing what to do. *Besides,* he thought, *what use are the sixty pesos I earned?* He looked for a public phone to call Julieta thinking they probably were all worried but couldn't find any that worked. He passed by a house where he saw a boy cleaning a pool. He looked through the bushes to get closer to him. To his astonishment, the boy surprised him because as he turned to look the other way, there he was, mere centimeters from his face.

Enrique was nineteen years old; he began cleaning pools since he was fourteen. They chatted for a while until Enrique invited him in. Lumerso took a deckchair and sprawled himself on it. He observed how easy it was to vacuum the crap from the pools. That would be a better job than putting up wallpaper, having to be careful with the wrinkles was the worst. He removed his clothes until he was only in the same underwear as the day before. In one dip he was in the water. He pulled at the tube of the vacuum Enrique was holding until he made him slip.

"There's no one in this house, right?" Lumerso asked.

Enrique shook his head no. They began to play like little kids without adult supervision. Enrique sank Lumerso's head with both hands, after he came back up for air, he asked:

"Are you a faggot?"

Lumerso hated the question. He didn't want to be gay anymore. He went back to the deckchair while Enrique continued cleaning the pool. Lumerso thought about staying in that house; after all, there was no one there. Enrique changed out of his work clothes. Once he was ready, he invited Lumerso to go with him to the next pool; he had to do two more, and then he asked him out for a meal. Lumerso followed him. He liked how direct Enrique was. He told him about the girlfriends he'd left behind in Tepoztlan, and how much he'd like to do something else, though he wasn't doing bad getting into pools every day.

When it was past five in the afternoon, they arrived to eat at the house of Lucia. She was the one in charge of assigning the jobs; she was also the owner of the house where the 'pool cleaners' lived. The woman took a look at Lumerso and felt he was a young guy who didn't know what to do with his life. She offered him to work alongside Enrique for now and added that he could also stay there; and if he did a good job, she'd find him a permanent spot. For the time being she'd pay him half.

"That's clear to me," Lumerso said with arrogance.

Lucia didn't take it personally. Lumerso was, after all, a teenager like all of them, full of hormones and about to blow up any moment.

Lumerso had been cleaning pools for three weeks when police officers patrolling the area detained him while he was entering a house. He looked scared, thinner than usual. His skin was dark and wrinkled. Lumerso explained to them that he was no thief. Neither of the patrolmen were interested in talking to him. They took him to the precinct and placed him like a delinquent in a tiny prison cell. There they kept him for three hours without even asking questions. Suddenly, Lumerso heard the sound of a male voice he'd been hearing his entire life. Ignacio entered the jail cell without saying a thing. He saw how dark-skinned Lumerso was. Told him he'd given them a scare, that his mother was in the waiting room. Ignacio didn't know if he should strike him, kiss him, or tell him how much he loved him. He did none of those. Told him to go see his mother. Josefina looked exhausted, haggard. She hugged him tightly, giving him a lot of kisses on his forehead.

"Whatever you wrote doesn't matter. Your father and I are really sorry about what happened with the journal," she said sweetly while looking at her husband. Josefina's words made Lumerso remember why he was in Cuernavaca.

Once they were home, he felt like he was in a strange place. He hadn't been there in almost four weeks. He remembered everything bigger. The house seemed to have more furniture. It definitely wasn't the bedrooms separated by plastic curtains where he arrived to sleep lately. Lumerso ran to a chair to sit. Jimena cornered him with questions; if he wanted something special to eat, where he'd been, why he never called. He didn't answer. Simply said he wasn't hungry. He went up to his bedroom. Josefina opened and closed the door to his bedroom every five minutes.

"Haven't escaped again, ma," Lumerso reacted while lying down on the bed.

Chapter XII

Escandon Neighborhood, 2019

It's cold. A rush of wind slips in through the terrace. Two men smoke by the staircase. Another goes down to the second floor. Today they want more than a hot body. It's not sex that they're looking for. They're looking for the company of a friend, a lover, a husband, someone that will want to listen to them. Today it doesn't look like a hookup house, but a place to meet a new interest. Christmas music comes from one of the improvised speakers. The owner has put up Christmas decorations, and a tree with lights and icicles; also, there's coffee, *atole* and hot chocolate by the foyer. And yet, the darkness remains there. No one wants to go in. Lumerso enjoys the space. A couple just arrived; they go right over him. They undress. The coats fall to the floor. Lumerso rushes to go into another room. A conversation calls his attention. Someone talks about what they'll do during the winter break: they'll spend it on the beach with the family. The conversation changes, they begin kissing. The night turns chilly. It's been a while since the doorbell rang. Lumerso goes down to the bottom floor. The basement is empty. Two others just arrived. They're half-naked. The second has decorated his penis with a metal ring. It's not hard. The one in trousers lays face down over an old bed and raises his buttocks. The second has a whip. He strikes him. Does it several times until his butt cheeks change color. On the upper floor a voyeur listens in. Decides to go down there. They take him by the arm, pull out his penis and make him suck the one being whipped. The three begin to enjoy themselves. A fourth man goes down in a hurry. He yells at them not to bang those two, that they're infected, that he knows them from the clinic. The one standing gets angry, yells at him to go away, for him not to be a busybody or he will fuck him up. They keep arguing until a shot is heard. The sound gets them all worked up. The guard had never used his gun until today. Some hide, others emerge from the holes, some others take off. Lumerso isn't scared. He cannot die twice.

"You either clear off... or I'm offing one of you!" the security man yells as he goes up the stairs.

They all look at each other now that the lights are on.

The men in leather go up. Christmas Eve is not the same anymore.

"Upstairs there's *atole*, hot chocolate and coffee... they even brought cookies," the guard says with studied sarcasm.

Lumerso has never seen him from the front until that moment. The man is a big one, with skin like sawdust and a square back. He always sees him from behind, in front of the bathroom when someone sucks him off. That's how he dodges the cameras. A man is lying face down, naked, waiting for another to arrive. The lights on the tree don't turn on. The cold intensifies. Lumerso sits before the naked man. Observes the loneliness in his eyes until that one cannot resist any more and starts to cry. The music cannot be heard anymore, it doesn't feel like a Christmas night any longer. The temperature keeps going down.

It's the same cold they felt at home the day Julieta returned from Switzerland. She was making fun of things saying that it was colder in Mexico than in Switzerland. His father replied that the houses there had heating; but here, even the blankets of Toluca could not help them handle the cold. They all sat at the table to enjoy the dinner prepared by Jimena before leaving to celebrate with her family. They followed the instructions to the letter of how to heat each dish. Josefina tried to do what she could, but Julieta seemed to have more experience than her. Ignacio, resting on the armchair, wanted to make use of that moment of happiness to talk to his son. Since his escapade in Cuernavaca, they rarely communicated. Whenever Ignacio tried to start a conversation, Lumerso simply ignored him.

"Classes at your college will begin soon?" Ignacio asked with great enthusiasm. Lumerso replied by asking his sister how did she came up with the idea of bringing him silk pajamas, because he'd have to wait until the summer to use them; and then he turned around and saw his father still waiting patiently for an answer. He answered curtly that it'd be on the second week of January. Ignacio wanted to ask another question but held back.

"Someone else wants ham?" Josefina asked.

They continued talking until past three in the morning, when Josefina and Ignacio went to sleep. Julieta stayed on the couch, talking with Lumerso. She told him that she was deeply sorry about the journal, but to understand that their parents were of a different generation and didn't know what to do with a gay son. Lumerso said that it didn't matter anymore, that he had other things in his mind. The journal thing being the least important of them. After hearing him out Julieta blurted what she'd been thinking all night:

"I'm not going to go back to school."

The news surprised Lumerso. Their parents had invested a lot of money in her, so that she'd graduate college with a degree. Julieta assured him that, at least for now, she'd look for a job in the government, until she found a boyfriend that could support her. Schools weren't for her. She could barely memorize absurd formulas she'd never use. Lumerso couldn't believe what his sister was saying. It was as if he were hearing his mother. After everything, now she didn't feel like keeping up with her studies. He felt betrayed by Julieta. Had he been in her place, he'd be living separate from his parents and they wouldn't have the conflicts that were now pulling them apart. He looked at Julieta thinking that it was the worst mistake of her life.

Those days it seemed that Lumerso always had money in his wallet. He himself was surprised that he wanted to keep studying. Maybe he didn't want to end up lost and without a life purpose. He said to Julieta that he managed to work two jobs that made him a good income, but that once she adapted once again to Mexico, he'd tell her about it. Julieta noticed he was thin; his cheeks were sunken. It wasn't the Lumerso she remembered.

"Tell me you're not on drugs!" Julieta exclaimed with unease.

Lumerso didn't answer. He shrugged and then went up the stairs. Julieta sensed that he wasn't doing well, that bad influences had changed him. She decided to open the present from Lumerso that he forgot to give her.

"From: Lumerso
To: Julieta, Merry Christmas!"

Julieta smiled. Patiently she unwrapped her present. Inside she found a pair of socks from when they were babies. One was Lumerso's, the other hers. Lumerso had found them in one of the trunks they kept in the attic. Julieta fell asleep on the couch until Josefina went down to prepare coffee.

Chapter XIII

Cuernavaca, 2007

Lumerso had been staying at the dorm in the outskirts of Cuernavaca for three days already. In that place, men of all ages arranged their mattresses on the floor however they could fit them. It was a room of about thirty square meters located on the grounds of a ranch. The walls were made of blocks, but unfinished. The garage was built as a parking lot for tractors. Since it wasn't being used, Lucia had it assigned as dorms for the pool cleaners. An iron door opened and closed only from the outside. The quarters were not located near any farmhouses. To get to Cuernavaca one needed to drive for about forty-five minutes. The same distance as from Mexico City. On top of that, it was a dirt road. The dorms were divided by plastic curtains. Inside the same room a metal sheet separated the latrine from the shower. Lumerso was assigned a mattress next to

Enrique. Most of the time he didn't sleep and when he managed to do it, he'd wake up screaming and drenched in sweat. He missed his parents, his house, his life. He wanted to call them, but his pride always shattered the idea. Enrique would feel Lumerso moving all night. He found him delicate, though he never got an answer as to whether or not he was a faggot. Sometimes Lumerso breathed deeply to make him believe he slept. He assumed that the others spied on him as well. Lumerso got used to stay up hearing his roommates snoring until way past midnight when he finally would fall asleep out of exhaustion.

At five in the morning they had to get up. And then it was such a rush that many times they just hustled to the bus without even cleaning themselves up. Enrique was the talkative kind, Lumerso had other things in his mind. He wasn't very enthused by his stupid stories. Just imagining that this might be his forever life made his stomach turn. He didn't think about returning to Mexico City for the time being, much less being humiliated by his father. He thought about writing another journal, but his current situation didn't lend itself to that.

The pool cleaners worked all day and then were brought back to Lucia, where they'd have something to eat. The earnings were small, but they enjoyed having a few beers in the backyard of whatever house was empty. Enrique was definitely a man of the streets. He was used to ordering people around and convincing everyone of whatever he wanted. Night after night he'd manage to persuade Lumerso to drink up to four beers. In several instances they would be completely smashed by the time they made it back to the dorms. Lumerso didn't have to fake in those occasions, it would take him only two minutes to fall asleep.

One night, after going back, while everyone slept, Enrique got close to Lumerso and began undressing him. They were both drunk. Lumerso turned away from him but didn't say a word. That night Enrique slept on top of him. The next day they went to work. Halfway through the morning Enrique mockingly mentioned to him that he said that his 'little one' was called Edgar. Lumerso wondered if the news of the paper might have already arrived in Cuernavaca.

"You called me that last night," Enrique indicated.

Lumerso didn't remember what had happened. Every day he found Enrique even more unpleasant. They kept working but Lumerso told him he wouldn't be going to eat with the crew, that he'd wait for them at the entrance to the highway. The next day he wanted to do the same. Enrique grabbed him by the arm with one hand and by the jaw with the other. As he pressed harder and harder, he said:

"Look, asshole, you're in this work because of me. If you want to be alone, you leave now."

Lumerso apologized, he blurted that there have been a lot of changes in such a short time. He promised they'd go to eat together and then do whatever he wanted.

"Whatever I want?" Enrique asked with a mocking grin.

Lumerso stayed quiet, regretting what he'd just said. He kept verifying the chemicals in the pool. Once finished, they were washing their faces in the bathroom when Enrique squeezed one of his butt cheeks.

"Good ass," Enrique said, smacking his ass while looking at the others.

Lumerso was extremely uncomfortable. Sex was the last thing on his mind. Not to mention the fact that he didn't like Enrique, not as a friend, not as anything. He'd love to leave, but what would he do then? Whatever savings he had weren't enough to get him anywhere and he had to take into consideration that the money came in and went out without pause.

He was almost done putting away the hose when Enrique grabbed him by the arm again to tell him:

"Look, little fucker, don't play with me. I know you like dick, and it is dicks what we're going to give you."

Lumerso didn't know what to say. He had a bad relationship with Lucia. She wasn't going to transfer him anywhere else. He thought about running away and leaving everything, but all his savings were at the dorm, inside his mattress. He studied Enrique talking to the others. He sensed he was their buffoon. Again, he thought about moving away and running but chose to distract himself. He was pulling his sandwich out of his bag when Enrique interrupted him:

"After we're done with the pools, we're all going for some beers."

Lumerso nodded yes. The best solution was to do what they wanted instead of trying to fight them. After all, it was a lot of them against only one.

They bought several six packs and took them to the ranch. Nightfall welcomed the group. A chilly wind set in for the evening. No one entered the dorms. Instead, they stayed outside. Enrique took a dry log and lit it on fire. Some dogs could be heard howling on the other side of the bushes. A few stars were shining. They all gathered around the fire. Lumerso said he was feeling ill, that it would be better if he didn't drink. That remark pissed off Enrique. He was looking forward to sleeping together drunk and having a good time. Enrique's tone was irritating. Lumerso knew he was gay but sleeping with one of those disgusting animals would be the worst he could do. Angry because of the situation, he took a beer and began to drink. Everyone piled on him until he would drink another. Lumerso went on until he drank seven more. He never thought he could get drunk so fast. After about an hour he almost fell over the ashes of the log. Between all of them they carried him and threw him on a mattress. They began to remove every piece of his clothing. Then Lumerso's thin body was set facing up. The man looked with envy at what Lumerso had between his legs. They decided to turn him around.

"I don't mind going first," said one with a belly so big it hunched his back. He opened his legs. Penetrated him. Lumerso let out a horrific scream. Enrique covered his mouth. The fat one moved his hips five times before coming. Lumerso began crying. It was his fault he was there, for being born gay. Why had he run away from his home? He felt that his head was somehow detached from his body. The pain in his rectum was overwhelming. Enrique immobilized his arms and took a sock to stuff it in his mouth. Regardless, another climbed upon him. He put on a condom and moved for a while before ejaculating. Enrique allowed Lumerso to move for a bit. But immediately the one they called Gorilla held him by the arms. It was Enrique's turn. He bit his back, his neck, pulled on his curls. He licked him everywhere. Opened his legs until he couldn't anymore. He penetrated him in one movement. Lumerso felt like he was dying. The effect of the alcohol seemed to make him more conscious of what was going on. Enrique kept enjoying himself until he came for a second time. Then another two followed. Lumerso was left lying down on the mattress where he'd already peed himself.

Lumerso fell asleep in that dirty mattress until the next day, when Enrique tried to wake him up. Lumerso wouldn't open his eyes so they left him there and locked the door. Lumerso yelled, but he knew no one would hear him. He remembered the second sandwich he had in his bag. He ate it. He couldn't believe what they'd done. He tried to go to the bathroom. Saw the blood running between his legs. Past six o'clock, Enrique arrived with his co-workers. He gave him a bag with some *chilaquiles*. Lumerso pushed them aside.

"Lucia says you should stay here until you're better."

"I'm fine... Can I go now?" Lumerso said angrily.

Enrique waited until Lumerso looked at him.

"If you'd behaved better, none of this would have happened to you," Enrique said smiling with cynicism.

Lumerso didn't answer. He stopped being the snobbish boy to become the submissive slave of these predators. While Enrique kept talking, he thought about all the different ways to eliminate them all, but ending his days in jail for homicide wasn't the best thing he could do with his life. It was better to forget that plan.

That day he spent every single minute thinking that he deserved this, that maybe he was guilty of his own actions. Being gay was an abomination, a disgrace, an imperfection, disgusting... and somehow, he should pay for pleasure with pain. Touching his cheek Enrique spoke:

"I hope you showered because tonight we're having round number two."

Lumerso took the bag with the *chilaquiles*. The men in the crew were all lying down on the mattresses. Apparently, the binge drinking of the day before and the working shift had tired them. Lumerso thought in a way of surviving. He subtly touched Enrique's leg like he once did with Antonio.

"What if it's just you and me?" Lumerso asked, controlling what he was really feeling.

Enrique replied that it'd be better not to do anything until the others fell asleep. He began looking at a comic magazine until he fell asleep. That night nothing happened.

Chapter XIV

Condesa Neighborhood, 2007

It was past nine thirty at night, but Lumerso had yet to return. When he went out for dinner or to the movies, it was the usual for him to let them know if he would be late returning. But this time he didn't. Josefina didn't want to alarm Ignacio. She thought that if she agitated him it could affect his heart condition. Josefina was trying to control her nerves. She went in and out of the garage to make sure the bicycle was there. Called the few phone numbers she kept of Lumerso's teachers. She phoned Edgar's mother. But no one had any news to give her. The police were her last option. They were all corrupt, the first thing they would ask for would be a bribe in order to begin the search.

That evening Ignacio returned at twenty minutes past eleven. Josefina was awake, she'd asked Jimena to stay. When he closed the door behind him

Ignacio saw the worried expressions in the faces of both women. He thought that something might have happened to Julieta, or perhaps to Lumerso himself. Josefina told him that Lumerso hadn't returned the whole day. She told him that their son hugged her before leaving, as if he were never going to see her again. Ignacio replied that she should leave those melodramas aside, that he must surely be upset and would spend the night at a friend's place. He didn't want any dinner. He apologized to Jimena and told her that he was sorry they'd made her stay, adding that she should go to sleep already because from where he stood, they were making a huge drama from nothing. Josefina decided to wait a little longer in the living room. Ignacio read the newspaper until he fell asleep in his armchair.

Lumerso didn't have many friends. After Edgar's departure no one visited him at home. Josefina thought about the journal and the stupid idea of burning it; surely, they could've found answers in its pages. She didn't know how to apologize for having read it; but even worse, for sharing it with Ignacio. She finished her cup of coffee. Poured more water into the coffee pot. It was five in the morning. Lumerso hadn't arrived yet. A little over past six she decided to wake Jimena up so they could go together to look for him. Perhaps someone had seen him the day before. Jimena said it was preferable to wait until the sun came out, since before that no one was awake. Josefina checked that the bicycle was still in the garage. It was half past eight in the morning when they heard Ignacio's footsteps. Neither of the two thought about preparing breakfast. Ignacio took a mug and poured himself some coffee, then he took a slice of bread and placed it in the toaster. It seemed strange to him that Lumerso hadn't returned. He didn't have the money to pay a hotel. He didn't think his savings would afford him any real-life expenses. He began to worry.

The women returned after having walked by Mexico Park and España Avenue until making it to Reforma Avenue. They didn't manage to ask anyone. Some were running to their jobs like mad people; while others ran like mad people to lose weight. Josefina sat beside Ignacio. She began to cry.

"Something must have happened to him for sure," she said.

Ignacio called Detective Delgado, a cop in charge of investigating matters of minors in the metropolitan area and its surroundings. After dialing several times, he managed to reach him.

Past five in the afternoon they still didn't have any news of Lumerso. Julieta was informed, but she knew there was nothing she could do from so far away. The school principal called to inform them that Lumerso had not attended classes for two days. This made Josefina worry even more. Ignacio began phoning investigators in state agencies he knew in Mexico, Hidalgo, and Morelos. Josefina got a hold of a recent picture of Lumerso and sent it to all the investigators using a fax machine they had in Ignacio's office.

That night they all stayed awake. They didn't know what to do anymore. Jimena didn't want to go back to the Buenos Aires neighborhood either. She felt guilty; after all, she was the one who found the infamous journal. After thinking it over for a while she said:

"What if you call Teran? Maybe Lumerso went there."

The idea didn't sound bad to Josefina. Ignacio only thought of the humiliation of explaining everything to his best friend. He rejected that plan.

Three weeks after Lumerso's disappearance, they were all thinking the worst. That he might have been kidnapped, that he was with human traffickers, and who-knows-where he might be. Someone called only to let them know that thus far there were no news regarding the case. The media didn't want to broadcast about yet another teenage runaway in Mexico City. Only the government accepted to place advertising in public transportation and broadcast news about the search on radio stations. Ignacio didn't know where to get more money from. He mortgaged the house to be able to pay the state investigators, keep covering Julieta's expenses and save money for the promised reward. He hadn't gone back to work. The state investigators kept asking for more and more money. Their savings ran out. There was no news about Lumerso. People called to say they'd seen him around downtown, or in the Zona Rosa, or as a homeless person in the Glorieta de los Insurgentes. All turned out to be lies. Ignacio was fed up with the fake news. He looked tired. A full beard covered half of his face. There was no life in that house since Lumerso's disappearance. Julieta would frequently call to tell them that she could go back, but they always replied that it wasn't worth it, that it was better if she stayed and finished her degree.

Detective Delgado arrived early on a Wednesday morning. He said he had good news, that luckily a lead had showed up after they offered a reward. The phone didn't stop ringing at the office, Delgado explained. A woman called to say she saw him in downtown Cuernavaca.

"We don't know anyone there," Josefina said puzzled.

Delgado went on to say that this woman believed she had seen him twice. That she said he was thinner, but it was the boy from the photograph. His hair was also longer.

"We need one more clue to send a patrol car to the area and we'll get your son back," Delgado said, tapping his bald head.

He said nothing else but waited to see if they'd offer him something more than a cup of coffee. Delgado remained seated. Ignacio pulled out the last two bills he had in his wallet. Josefina thanked him for the news. A small ray of hope shined in her eyes. She called Jimena to tell her he was alive, that they had found him. Jimena replied that she was already sure that that would be the case and added that a young man like Lumerso doesn't go missing in the middle of the night. She added that Our Lady of Guadalupe had answered their prayers.

A week later, Lumerso was on his bed, thinking which might be the best way to escape. He wasn't the same person anymore. His thoughts were different. He remembered everything he'd lived through in Cuernavaca. He was afraid his parents would send him back to his endless sessions with the shrink. He thought of Enrique but eliminated the thought before it was fully formed. He was interrupted by his mother's voice, asking if he wanted something to eat. An erotic gay movie filled the half-screen. He'd just bought a one-way ticket to Acapulco. He turned off the computer and went down for dinner.

Chapter XV

San Cosme Metro Station, 2010

Lumerso felt wind rushing behind his back. It was three months to the day of his father's passing. It was also his birthday. But it was not a happy one. He hated his job at the bus station and when he was at home, he barely if ever left the apartment at Romita. He started to think what the best way would be to make some money. On the website *Manhunt*, a stranger invited him to a gay bathhouse in the city. He didn't want to answer. Though he did feel curiosity about going to a place where he could get in touch with other gay people, people who would accept him, but more importantly, who felt the same way. It made no sense for him to turn twenty and remain holed up. Since his father's death everyone's lives in the family had gone to hell. The money left in his dad's bank account had not even been enough to cover the funeral expenses. On top of everything, the bank surprised them when they foreclosed on the house and evicted them. Life was over for his father, but not for him, even if it felt that bad. Ignacio was dead, and with that he'd been released of all of his family's responsibilities. He wanted to forgive him, but the memories of his actions kept him from it.

He found his mother sitting in the kitchen. She hadn't touched the oatmeal, nor the apple Julieta served her earlier. He kissed her forehead, telling her she was still the most beautiful woman in the world. Josefina didn't react. That was how she lived since Ignacio's death. Hers was no longer a faraway look, it was a look between life and death. Lumerso thought about taking the bike, but the bankers had snatched even that. They'd taken everything, though they didn't manage to seize some personal possessions. Julieta filed a lawsuit against the government to recover their belongings, but she didn't know how long it would be before they'd hear back or saw results. Ignacio didn't pay the mortgage for over a year; the worst was that his life insurance had gone unpaid too.

Lumerso wasn't used to taking public transportation. Before, he would take his bike or his father's car, which they no longer had. It was past one in the afternoon when he bought the subway ticket in the Chilpancingo station. The place was jammed with vendors. He told the woman selling him the ticket that today was his birthday. Her expression didn't change. He made it to San Cosme station. Walked until reaching a perpendicular street where he found the baths. There was no sign on the outside. The man at the door asked where he wanted to go. Lumerso didn't know what to say, he answered to the heated pools.

"There's two of them, general public or single use?" the man asked. He sounded annoyed.

Lumerso didn't know if it was him, or everyone was in a bad mood. No one smiled at him like before anymore. He just wanted to know the place. He decided to go to the general public pool.

It was an old place. Unkempt. Men walked around covered only with a white towel tied to their waists. They filed down a wet and dirty hallway. He went up to an enclosure where he waited until they offered him a room the size of a prison cell. *It'd be horrible to die in a place like this and be locked up forever*, he thought. The rooms were really tiny, the air felt stale and he didn't see any windows. After about five minutes, he decided to go out with the towel tied to his waist just like everyone else. He felt the eyes on him.

Lumerso was slim but his muscles showed perfectly on his body. He kept his hair long. A thick beard made him look more manly. The others noticed that he'd never been there before. He kept walking until finding a big steam room, another middle-size and one last, smaller one, which he couldn't figure out what it was for. He went into the big one that smelled like the herbs Grandma Victoria used for her breathing problems. He couldn't see a thing. A tanned man was lying face up. Another, kneeling on the ground, was giving him oral sex. A strong cloud of steam was coming out of a pipe on one side. Another man, thin, with white skin, masturbated while perversely watching everything. Just looking at that made

Lumerso feel sick. But he wanted to be cool. He removed his towel and the thin man tried to grab his penis. Lumerso took his hand off him. He stood up and walked to another sauna. The room was over fifty-one degrees Celsius. He loved the heat there. This time he didn't take off his towel. He placed himself before the boiler to feel how the heat went through his body and opened all his pores. He enjoyed feeling his body beginning to sweat. His face turned red. He heard someone call his name.

"Lumerso!"

Despite the heat Lumerso's muscles froze. He didn't have the faintest idea of who was talking to him. The voice said his name again. It was Enrique, the only person who, amid more than twenty million people in the city, he never thought to find there. He approached him. He looked scrawny but at the same time strong and manly. He sported a new mustache that made him look older. He hugged him asking why the hell he left without saying goodbye, but fuck, how good was fate that it made them find each other again. Lumerso wanted the earth to open in that moment and swallow him, end him once and for all. Never did he think to find anyone he knew in this place, much less Enrique. He didn't understand the universe. Why did it do such things to him? Lumerso heard him. He didn't want to say anything. Enrique grabbed him by the arm, like he did countless times in the past. Took him to a smaller place. A burst of steam came through the floor and some old eucalyptus leaves placed over the wood. A light came in when the door opened. Enrique threw it open quickly but couldn't close it from the inside. Lumerso thought about kicking him in the testicles, just like he planned to infinite times before. The door opened. A man entered. Lumerso smiled. He turned to face Enrique, who had his back to him. It was Edgar. Lumerso was incredulous at his presence. The universe hadn't played dirty, after all. Edgar understood that Lumerso was busy, opened the door to get out.

"Help me!" Lumerso cried out in a desperate tone.

Edgar pulled him by the arm, telling him they should go somewhere else. Enrique punched Edgar in the face to get him to leave. Lumerso finally gave a good kick to Enrique in the testicles. Enrique fell to the floor. A man who was just getting in ran to call security. Enrique writhed in pain, clutching his bruised balls. Lumerso and Edgar ran out of the steam room. They locked themselves in a bathroom. No one saw them go out or in. Edgar asked if they had cameras in that place. Lumerso replied that it was the first time he was there. When two guards and a man dressed in white approached Enrique, he didn't want to say anything. He just stood, waiting for Lumerso and his friend in front of the locker rooms. Neither of them came out. They remained locked up in the bathroom for over an hour.

"It's our destiny to meet in public places!" Edgar exclaimed, laughing his head off.

Lumerso chuckled as well. He was so happy to see him. He told him that it was his birthday today and meeting up with him was the best gift. Edgar asked him who that guy was, Lumerso answered that it was a long story, and not worth it. It was four in the afternoon when they got out. Edgar said he was starving. He wanted to invite him to a special place where they could celebrate. On the street, in front of the baths, Enrique awaited them. He looked at them intensely, following them with his eyes. Edgar had his car parked two blocks away. Before getting to the parking lot he felt a blow to his neck. Lumerso turned and punched him in the nose. Enrique was less slim. Edgar had a gym body; he was muscled and strong. He kept hitting him until a patrol car with two cops showed up. Edgar wanted to run, but a policeman followed until he caught up with him. He handcuffed him. The other one already had Lumerso handcuffed. Enrique had been left unconscious on the sidewalk. They put Edgar and Lumerso in the patrol car; they ended in the Public Prosecutor's Office.

"We always end up in close-up spaces," Lumerso said, more serious this time.

They locked them up for three days until Julieta and Edgar's mother went to get them. They talked a lot. Told each other how hard it was for Edgar to leave. Lumerso told him about what happened in Cuernavaca, and who Enrique was. Edgar felt pain for having abandoned him.

"Maybe none of this would have happened if we'd fixed things," Edgar said without thinking about it.

The expressions on Julieta's and Edgar's mother's faces weren't exactly of happiness. Edgar, upon climbing into his mother's van, saw how Julieta and Lumerso waited for the bus nearby. His mother refused to take them. Julieta said that they were lucky, that the so-called Enrique was married. He didn't want to accuse them of anything either; besides, no one on the block saw a thing.

"You were lucky this time."

Lumerso wanted to take her hand to express how grateful he was, but Julieta's look frightened him.

Chapter XVI

Condesa Neighborhood, 2003

That day Josefina was excited. She had not seen her mother, Victoria, in more than fifteen years. She left the country and moved to Toronto. In between postcards, changed phone numbers, addresses, she no longer knew where she was or had any clue about her latest adventures. Lumerso didn't know much of his grandmother either, with the exception of the pictures of her youth that his mother kept over her nightstand. Josefina talked little about her. Didn't understand why she left to find a love outside of Mexico, when the most romantic men were in the country. Victoria followed a dream, an impossible love, a love, nonetheless. That changed a little after she flew away from her own family. After a while Josefina grew tired of hearing who was her new lover. Every week or month it was a different beau. After a while she stopped asking. The last known location of her mother was New Zealand and now she was surprised when she said she was flying in from Sydney. She didn't know how to conceal her mother's lifestyle from Ignacio.

Last week they took Julieta to the airport. Today they were picking up grandma. Everyone constantly boarded airplanes and Lumerso watched them from afar. How was it possible that he'd never gotten on a plane? He was already tired of his father's promises that one day they'd go to Orlando and the fabulous Magic Kingdom. Nothing but lies.

Ignacio made a brief stop at the entrance of international arrivals and let his family get off the car. Then, he went to park the vehicle. Lumerso asked his mother how she'd recognize grandma since she would surely look much older than before. Josefina answered that she will know instinctively because even when people age, fatten up or slim down their essence remains and that's how we recognize them, was her explanation. Lumerso was left pondering on his mother's words; that was how he remembered his dog Oliver, as if they were still always together.

Before Ignacio returned from parking the car, a slim woman with golden hair showed up with an endless number of suitcases. Lumerso thought that all that could not fit in the car; and when he turned to his mother, he saw her making some faces he'd never seen before on her.

They hugged and greeted each other loudly stating how good each of them looked. Lumerso knew they were lying; people always said nice words like that, but he knew they were not telling the truth; most of the time they looked much older or larger or skinnier.

Grandma Victoria was tall and despite her golden-colored hair what stood out the most about her was her incredibly aged skin. Lumerso greeted her with a handshake; to him, that woman was a stranger.

Ignacio was annoyed when he made it back to meet his family and realized that because of the luggage, now he would have to pay for an additional cab on top of the parking fee. He also realized he could've gotten away with just waiting curbside instead of parking. He went back for the car. They all started to walk behind Ignacio. A porter followed them, helping with the luggage. They kept praising each other until grandma asked for Julieta. Josefina answered that it was better for her to study outside of Mexico, eventually she'd be able to marry a wealthy man. Meanwhile, Lumerso observed his grandma's every movement; he felt he was like her. He wanted to ask her so many questions: What had she done during all that time? How come she never came back to visit his mother? Now his grandmother returned with all that luggage to start over in a country she no longer knew. He felt pity for her. Surely some kind of tragedy must have happened to her, Lumerso determined.

They loaded grandma's luggage in the taxi but decided to go together in Ignacio's car. The Saturday traffic moved slowly. From time to time Lumerso would turn and look out the back window to make sure the taxi was still following them. Ignacio had his doubts as well, he was almost sure at any moment the driver would make a different turn and vanish with all the luggage. He did insist the two women should travel in the cab, but grandma said things like that never happened to her. Keeping an eye on the taxi driver, after almost an hour on the road Ignacio said that they would have made it to Cuernavaca already. Lumerso didn't understand, but he liked the sound of that name. After a little more than two hours of driving the taxi parked in front of the house.

Julieta's bedroom was arranged to receive grandma. They had taken her single bed and replaced it with a queen size. They all helped with the luggage and soon enough grandma was drinking a tall glass of whiskey on the rocks, which, according to her, was the best remedy for jetlag. Apparently, no matter how many glasses she had she could never get over that. Lumerso asked what jetlag was. Grandma explained that it was a feeling of wooziness caused by changing time zones when traveling from one country to another one. Lumerso didn't understand what she meant by that. He couldn't imagine people going from one place to the other and getting sick because of their clocks showing different times. This jetlag didn't make any sense to him.

In the kitchen, Jimena was teeming with vitality. She'd finished cooking a good Mexican meal to welcome Grandma Victoria. She'd found some fresh nuts to prepare *chiles en nogada*, a *cochinita pibil*, and a *pastel azteca*. Grandma Victoria was quite pleased. And since the bottle of whiskey was already half-finished, Ignacio pulled out a bottle of Don Julian and sat at the foot of the coffee table.

"To Grandma Victoria, a woman of worlds," Ignacio said passionately. No one knew if he was being sarcastic or genuine. Lumerso tried a bit of tequila but found the taste awful. He couldn't understand why adults insisted on drinking it.

After that wonderful meal, grandma wanted to go for a walk. Josefina asked Lumerso to take her to the park and show her the way people took their little dogs out for a walk in the neighborhood. Everything was very European-style or as if they were leaving in East New York. They walked down Amsterdam Avenue to Michoachan Avenue. Grandma Victoria was surprised at the large amount of coffee shops, restaurants and dogs that now engulfed Condesa. When they were on their way back Lumerso stared at his grandmother, who looked tired.

"You know I'm gay," Lumerso said very matter of fact.

Grandma Victoria replied that she didn't know, but that it was nothing shameful. That people were born that way and that they should be able to do anything with their lives. She explained to him that many people in the world were: Michelangelo, Leonardo Da Vinci, Oscar Wilde and many more that she didn't remember in that moment. Lumerso didn't have the slightest idea of who those people were. He confessed her that his parents had already made him go to several sessions with the psychiatrist. He also told her that he felt alone and that no one understood him, except for his friend Edgar, who was like him but felt sick to have been born like that.

"I will have none of that nonsense," Grandmother Victoria cut him abruptly. "You're gay; or better yet, homosexual."

A woman that was walking with her two dachshunds looked at her terrified.

Grandma Victoria kept talking. She said that she had a lot of gay friends and that when she lived in

Canberra, she threw parties just to invite them. She loved hanging out with them because they were very funny people, and, better yet, they had exquisite taste. They kept talking until Lumerso found himself opening the house's gate. After that, grandma went upstairs to sleep.

Grandma Victoria had been only a few days in Mexico City when she discovered that everything annoyed her. She developed a dry cough that nothing would soothe. The doctor placed her on oxygen so she could breathe at night. Lumerso spent a lot of time in her room keeping her company. Sometimes, when the days were clear, they'd go on walks to the park, but then the cough would worsen. The stench coming from the park aggravated her medical condition. Josefina lived in anguish. Ignacio asked why she didn't stay over there, instead of coming to mortify them. They talked about the possibility of admitting her into a nursing center. She was terrified by the vendors with the loudspeakers. She didn't understand why they had to go by all the time. Lumerso listened to her. Fed her the odd soups that Jimena prepared. He listened to the stories of François, Henry, Vermont, and many other lovers she had around the world. She told him the story of why she left Mexico. Lumerso never got tired of listening to Grandma Victoria. Her stories carried a parallelism with the life he dreamt of having.

When Grandma Victoria was twenty-nine, she got impregnated by Carlos. He was engaged but called the engagement off. He never loved her anyway. Life was a nightmare for both. They bought an apartment around the Roma neighborhood and they lived there for twelve years until some robbers broke into the house and shot Carlos dead. For several years she lived there with Josefina, until she left to study. She recovered her freedom. Met Gilberto, whom she loved blindly, and who loved her too. One day he arrived home full of Mexican manhood; he ordered her to never cut her hair. Victoria's hair at the time was curly, long, and brown. The next day she went to the beauty parlor and returned looking like a trainee soldier. She couldn't stand anyone to tell her how to dress or what to do with her life. Gilberto packed his bags that same day. Never again did she heard from him. She too, made the decision to leave, to go somewhere else. She wanted to be the free woman she always wished to be. She sold the Roma apartment. Met Pier, a Canadian, in a bar downtown. Four weeks later she moved with him to Canada. By that time Josefina had already met Ignacio and they had just gotten married. That was how Grandma Victoria's life outside of Mexico began. Lumerso, in between coughs and sips of water colored with whiskey, listened incredulous to his grandmother's stories. At one in the afternoon the soap opera marathon would begin. Right before, Lumerso would stand up and close the curtains. He watched one or the other without paying attention to them. He wondered if lying belly up on the bed, with his eyes closed, was the best way to die.

One March 12th in 2005, Grandma Victoria passed away. Lumerso cried like never before. That night he slept in the bed she once occupied.

That morning he'd gone to school like he did every day. Upon returning he asked his mother and Jimena if they'd fed grandma because he hadn't earlier. He immediately went up to the bedroom with a tray with bean soup and a glass of carrot juice. He pulled out the bottle of whiskey and added a few drops. He opened the door. Saw her sleeping. He went to open the curtains, tried to wake her up, but he could not. Lumerso sat beside her. He tried the juice. He did not understand why grandma liked such strange blends. He cried for a long while. Turned on the TV. The *telenovela* "*El amante de María*" had just started. Then he stepped out of the room and yelled:

"Mom, grandma died."

Josefina and Jimena almost broke the dishes they were cleaning in the kitchen and ran upstairs. Lumerso's eyes were puffy. He was tired of crying. Josefina hugged him, but she didn't shed a single tear.

Chapter XVII

Roma Neighborhood, 2012

Lumerso left work at the bus station feeling very tired. He had not seen Genaro since that time he took him to eat *tacos* and then to the hotel. Life seemed to filter not only through a strainer, but through a single channel, without going anywhere. Straight timelines bored him, he despaired with the repetitiveness of life, of this life he had chosen. That Saturday he lay down on the bed to explore the *Manhunt* website on his cellphone. The associate degree at the *Tecnologico* seemed ever farther from his reality. He had time to spare. He left work not knowing what to do or where to go. The membership to the swimming club was canceled. The bicycle was still held by the bank. Julieta lost hope of recovering their computers, cellphones, or any other seized possession. There was nothing left to do but locking himself at home. Josefina was no company. She spent whole days in the darkness, watching the turned off TV. She would get upset when Lumerso turned it on. Julieta had lost her light. She didn't have a boyfriend. Josefina's plans got lost in her empty head. Julieta kept growing fatter. Lumerso hadn't made any friends when he was at college before. The few friends from high school went to other places in Mexico or the United States. A few sent him requests through *Facebook*, but he deleted them. He was ashamed of his life. While they took selfies skiing or in the Magic Kingdom; he was left stagnant in a life he refused to understand. After going through a list of men profiles in *Manhunt*, he was surprised by a text message:

Hello!

He didn't recognize who it was. Wanted to block him. He opened again the *Facebook* website. He wanted to write in his wall how boring his life was. Another message interrupted him again:

I'd like to see you. I have a proposal, you interested????

He didn't recognize the number. Just as he was about to block it, another message came in:

I'm Genaro. Remember me?

Lumerso focused on the pain that guy caused him, it was so bad it kept him awake for a week. He wanted to block him, tell him that he was a sexual pervert, a disgusting person, but he didn't write any of that. He decided to answer him:

What's up...?

Genaro didn't answer for ten minutes. Lumerso was almost certain he wanted to do the same. While he waited, he thought about the money. It would be nice to get some since his next check was still a week away.

Genaro asked him for naked pictures: front and back. Lumerso took them and sent them. But the cellphone he'd bought on the street wasn't good at all. The pictures took a while to get to the other side. After twenty minutes, Genaro answered:

Can I call you?

Seconds later, Genaro was on the phone. He said he'd pay him about three thousand pesos for a sex session, but he had to do it with several men, perhaps two or three at once.

"Do they all have it like yours?" Lumerso asked, worried.

Genaro proudly replied that no, no one had it like him. Lumerso didn't want to commit himself and then regret it. He asked several questions. He still wasn't convinced but they arranged to meet in a park in the Reforma Avenue in a couple of hours.

Past ten o'clock, Genaro was already waiting for him. The coffee shop was full. There was only a chair left for Lumerso. Genaro offered him an ice cream. Said it was the best food for before and after sex. It had sugar, so it gave you energy without the need to eat anything heavy, Genaro rambled. Lumerso replied it was alright, that he had dinner already. Everything about that man bothered him. He represented a world he didn't understand; and yet, it seemed that now he was getting even closer. He wanted to run like he did during therapy sessions with the shrink. But running away in that moment would be fleeing from his own destiny. Genaro was looking at him with lust. He didn't seem to care about Lumerso's tormented face. Genaro repeated that they would have the best of times. Lumerso didn't listen, he observed a table with several gay guys laughing loudly and dressed in the latest fashions. He, on the other hand, was wearing stained jeans, a white t-shirt and dirty sneakers. He didn't understand why he once again found himself before that man. Just looking at him caused him revulsion. He came to think that it wasn't the need for money but rather a strange pleasure what attracted him. Genaro finished explaining things with verbal clauses. All he was missing was presenting him a written contract. Everything was said. The money he'd get upon entering the basement, but not before. He could use poppers, marijuana, or whatever other substance he wanted. He'd bring everything necessary. He asked if he was clean. Lumerso answered that he'd just taken a shower. Genaro looked at him disconcerted. He didn't want accidents mid-act. He recommended that he shower again and get a good scrubbing. He'd wait for him at the address he'd given him at exactly five minutes before midnight.

At 11:55 p.m. Lumerso was waiting for them in front of the place Genaro indicated. He was carrying his backpack with a few belongings, including a pair of flip-flops and silk underwear that he had to buy at Genaro's request. He gave his mother a kiss before leaving. Sent a text to Julieta to let her know he wouldn't be back until the next day.

La Casona was a mysterious place. There was no number on the outside. The glass on the windows was painted black. A bright white lightbulb illuminated a small dark door. Genaro touched the intercom for several seconds until the door opened. Lumerso found it strange that they had to climb stairs. He thought that the place would be in the house where they rang the doorbell. When they arrived at the landing of the stairs another door opened on its own. A guard with a smiling face received them. The entrance was like a market stand. They sold condoms, lubricants, leather whips, cigarettes, beer, briefs, bras, and panties. Genaro asked Lumerso if he needed something. Lumerso shook his head. They asked for his ID to corroborate that he was not a minor. Genaro went inside without saying anything. Three men were waiting for them in a small living room. Lumerso greeted them icily. The men looked at him brazenly, like dogs after finding a piece of meat. He could feel them drooling.

Lumerso removed his clothes until he was left in his underwear. Lumerso wasn't short, but not tall either, his back and his legs showed athletic muscles. He was wearing white silk underwear with blue stripes on the sides. It was so tiny, though, it made no sense: most everything was left uncovered. He handed his backpack to a man without eyebrows seating behind the bars in the entry area. He handed him a ticket he'd need afterwards to claim his belongings; otherwise, he'd have to leave the place naked. Lumerso nodded. They went down and up the stairs, through a hallway, then another, until reappearing at an open space. It was the terrace. They went then through a bathroom, where they asked Lumerso if he wanted to go before going to the basement. Lumerso declined, said he was okay, that he'd gone already. One of them gave him a hard spank. Grabbed his lifeless cock. The anticipation for what was about to happen was making Lumerso shake.

"Good thing we're not using it," the man said, letting go of his penis.

They went past hallways and rooms with no lights. Men of all ages exited and entered the rooms. Lumerso felt dread. How the hell did he get to this point in his life? Another guy going up squeezed his penis again. Lumerso couldn't believe that in Mexico City there could be a place like that. They kept walking until they made it to a classy staircase. The space was open and comfortable. Leather furniture set the tone in the living room. Naked men sucked penises, others enjoyed penetrations, others just watched while they masturbated. Lumerso thought that maybe he'd like to watch. He didn't want to fuck with one of these men he didn't know. He thought about going up the stairs and getting the hell out of that place. They kept going down until they made it to the basement. Genaro pulled out three thousand pesos in six five-hundred bills and handed them to Lumerso. He didn't know what to do with the money. Didn't even have where to put it. He thought about the socks. Placed it in the center of the sole of the foot. They went in. Genaro was carrying a bag with dildos, poppers, lubricants and even a first-aid box. He gave Lumerso two pills without explaining what they were for. Lumerso swallowed them as best he could with a shot of tequila. The short man bent down like a pig to bite Lumerso's underclothes. He pulled at them but couldn't tear them. Lumerso got a lash. That was nothing compared to what he'd be feeling later. The other decided to rip the underwear. He threw it to the floor. Genaro tied Lumerso by his arms and legs and hung him upside down. The short one kept sucking his dick like a calf, he wanted to give him an erection. Lumerso wasn't responding. Genaro began to lubricate him. Another went for his lips. Licked him.

Pulled at his hair until he got his tongue inside Lumerso's mouth. They smoked pot. The short one filled his mouth with pot smoke. Then he put his lips on Lumerso's penis. Afterwards he inhaled the magic liquid, as Genaro called it. Lumerso felt like losing himself. He stopped being himself. Unknown sensations made him shudder. He surrendered his body for them to do what they wanted. Others arrived to watch, but no one else could touch him. Genaro was the first to penetrate him. The huge penis entered Lumerso like a knife splitting his body apart. Genaro yelled, he enjoyed it. The pig sucked Lumerso's now hard penis. The other one climbed on top of him. He gave him more weed to smoke. Lumerso continued to be in ecstasy. He'd gone into a trance. He thought himself possessed by demons or vengeful spirits; someone he couldn't see but definitely feel. He thought he could see ghosts awaiting him. A few hours ago, he was at his place, bored, with nothing to do. Now he was there, servicing these men, for the amount of money that he kept in the sole of his foot. Lumerso didn't feel pain. The drugs controlled him. His body felt relaxed, open, as if it were someone else's. All of them kept getting pleasure from him. One made him swallow his semen. Two more came inside his anus. Genaro covered his back in semen. Lumerso remained there, lying down. He didn't know how many times the pig had made him come either. He was unconscious. The ones who paid began leaving the crowded space. Others came in to enjoy him without him finding out.

Lumerso managed to wake up after ten in the morning. Wilfredo found him tied up. The place was empty. He felt pity for the boy. Wondered how much they must have paid for him to let them do such filthy things. "Money does everything in this country," was what Wilfredo repeated constantly. Lumerso opened his eyes. He saw a gray-haired man untying him. He asked about his clothes.

"You can wash over there. Your clothes are upstairs," Wilfredo said indifferently. "Do you have the ticket?" he asked him.

Lumerso remembered that he'd put it away along with his money in the left sock. He couldn't walk. His legs were shaking. He couldn't feel his arms. He thanked Wilfredo for taking away the ropes.

It was a beautiful Sunday morning. The streets were empty. The Escandon neighborhood was clear of street vendors. A blue sky wrapped around the city. A couple of clouds said their farewells in the distance. The sun was taking its time to get up high. Lumerso didn't see any of that. He was tired, dazed, disoriented. Every tiny muscle in his body ached. He didn't know which way to go. He remembered that he no longer lived in Condesa. It would have been best to stay home, instead of answering that message. He had money now but working like he did with those men would get him killed overnight. He smelled of a disgusting mix of everything. He would've given anything for a shower at that moment. He felt ashamed of going home. How would he ever be able to look his mother in the face, or his sister, after what he'd done? He was no longer Lumerso De la Torre, he was another man, one he did not know or recognized. When he wanted to cross Patriotismo Avenue he heard a young man talking to him. He yelled out to him several times. Lumerso was ignoring him. Suddenly the guy stepped in front of him.

"I'm Erick, we met early on a Sunday?"

Lumerso heard him, but each word felt like a blow to his head. Erick wouldn't stop talking. Said he was thrown out of a dive for falling asleep in the latrine. He kept talking about everything he'd done the night before. It didn't compare with what Lumerso experienced. Until he heard:

"... and then I ended at La Casona."

"You were there?" Lumerso asked.

Lumerso tried to remember some faces, but there were more than a hundred men in that place. Of all kinds: big, small, thin, fat, white, dark. He could never remember anyone's face, even if he had him before him. Finally, Erick said:

"I do remember you; you were the guy at the basement, one of those who arrive after midnight. I've done it a few times, but it takes weeks to recover." Erick kept telling him that it was the worst trick anyone could do for so little money, and that he charged five thousand, but that they no longer asked him because he made his own rules. Lumerso couldn't believe what he was hearing.

"Let's go for a *birria*!" Erick continued without stopping the chattering.

They ate and talked about everything they'd like to do with their lives, though Lumerso thought that at least for the time being he'd have to continue with what he'd gotten into. Erick said he lived in a rooftop room around the Juarez neighborhood, and that if he wanted, they could go sleep there.

"No sex!" Lumerso cried out.

"None," Erick answered.

They seemed to have no secrets. They knew each other just as they were. Neither of them had money, or designer clothes to show off. This guy without any weirdness to account for caught Lumerso's interest. They slept until late at night, when Lumerso woke up to the sound of his cellphone. It was Julieta. They talked for a few minutes and he told her he wouldn't be back until the next day. Erick kissed Lumerso on the lips. Neither of them wanted anything more. They fell asleep again. Didn't wake up until the morning, when Erick remembered that he had to go pick up the taxi he worked.

"See you later?" Lumerso asked.

Erick noticed the dark bags under Lumerso's eyes, wanted to ask him until what time he'd be at the bus station; but before he had the chance, Lumerso was already telling him he wasn't going back. A week later he went for his last check. The office assistant told him that because he left his post without notice she had nothing for him.

Chapter XVIII

Washington, D.C., 2002

Edgar's mother got up early. Santiago, her husband, had been traveling across the United States for over a month already. Sometimes he spent months without returning. Magdalena and Edgar were already used to Santiago's absence. The business of selling pharmaceutical products kept going splendidly, despite the difficult economic situation the country faced. Santiago's trips were tiring, but they allowed for a comfortable life for him and his family.

With her arms crossed tightly over her chest, Magdalena anxiously watched Edgar from the kitchen; she was trying to figure out the best way to tell him the news. Sonia, their housemaid, was at their flat roof hanging clothes. Magdalena watched her son scarf down his Mexican-style eggs. It looked like he didn't even stop to breathe. When Edgar was about to bite into the last piece of *tortilla,* she spoke to him:

"You're going to Washington with your uncle Guillermo." The last bite almost got stuck in his throat. He took a gulp of milk, stood up and walked aggressively past his mother to throw his dishes into the sink. He didn't want to say something he could regret later. Instead, he decided to go outside. He was irate. Whenever something happened at school or in his life, they wanted to send him off to the house of some relative, like he and his problems were some kind of package you can get rid of whenever things got out of hand. He couldn't even remember what happened the last time they tried using that lever to send him to visit his father's sister, Aurora, in Chihuahua. It didn't matter. She did not want the responsibility so the whole thing died on its own. But now his uncle Guillermo was a high-ranking diplomat. Ever since he was named Mexican Ambassador to the United States, they wanted to visit as much as possible. First, it was for Thanksgiving; then for winter break, when he'd just moved; then they returned to tour George Washington's homestead, followed by a three-day trip to New York. They made Edgar visit universities, as they were trying to get him excited about getting a college degree in the capital city of the United States. Edgar simply didn't like Washington, D.C. He hated visiting freezing buildings and museums that seemed to never end. He liked the national zoo, but they never visited it in the summer, the only time when they'd would've been able to see all the exhibits.

Edgar took his bicycle and started to get as far away from his house as he could. He was on his way to his school when he saw Lumerso, but instead of going across the street to meet him, he ignored him. When they made it to class, they did not say a word to each other and put many lines of desks in between themselves.

Lumerso left in a hurry as soon as he heard the recess bell ringing. Edgar stayed back to finish a reading for the next class. He couldn't concentrate. He wanted to tell everything to his best friend, but he was afraid Lumerso would propose some idiotic idea, like moving to Cancun. He pulled out an apple and a ciabatta bread that his mother put in his schoolbag.

After half an hour, Lumerso returned. They sat together for a while without talking. When the bell rang again Lumerso returned to the same seat where he'd been before.

That same afternoon Edgar found his mother waiting for him in the living room.

"You're leaving in three weeks," Magdalena said firmly.

Edgar went into his bedroom. He didn't come out until nine that night. Sonia had gotten tired of waiting for him and went to sleep. He quickly ate a dish made of ground meat and rice and a side of beet salad. When he was about to return to his bedroom his mother caught up to him.

"It's for your own good... That boy's going to make you a 'little faggot' like him."

Calling his best friend 'faggot' was the worst his mother could have ever said.

"We're not 'faggots', we're gay," Edgar yelled back, he was furious. Magdalena didn't expect her own son to recognize that he was sick too. She followed him to his room, but Edgar slammed the door in her face and locked it from the inside. It stayed that way until the following day.

Magdalena didn't say any more on the matter, and Edgar didn't want to ask. He continued attending school hoping that everything would reach an agreeable resolution that didn't involve national or international send-offs. The idea of leaving for a country he did not like, aside from having to study a language that wasn't his own, made his soul feel sick. He didn't need to leave Mexico to fix the so-called identity crisis his mother spoke of.

One night, after dinner, Lumerso arrived at Edgar's place without warning. Magdalena ran to the door to try to get rid of him, but Edgar got in her way and invited his friend in under the guise of drinking some Orangeade.

Glass in hand, Edgar observed him as if trying to memorize each of his features. He saw Lumerso's sad eyes and that beautiful smile that dazzled him every time he saw it. He thought about telling him that he loved him, that they would be a couple when they grew up, but his mother's voice interrupted him.

"If you're going to work you need to do it on the dining room table," Magdalena yelled from the hallway.

Lumerso and Edgar did as Magdalena asked and were together solving math problems until close to midnight. Edgar heard his mother moving around at the TV room. He knew she watched TV on mute to spy on them and hear what they were saying.

When it was fifteen minutes to midnight, Magdalena came around and loudly stated that it was time to go to sleep. At that point Edgar decided it was better to leave things with Lumerso there. He thought it was pointless. In a few days he'd be living in his uncle's house. He wanted to tell Lumerso that he wouldn't be seeing him at school anymore, that he loved him, but above all, for him to forgive him. He didn't dare. Just thinking that his mother might hear him made him panic.

Edgar continued attending classes until one day Lumerso saw him leaving school with his mother. It was the first time anyone picked him up. A light drizzle was starting to fall. Edgar shrugged in defeat and silently walked alongside his mother. Lumerso looked on until he lost them in the fog. Truth is that Edgar wanted to explain, to say a proper goodbye, but his mother forbade him from telling Lumerso or anyone else that he was moving to Washington, D.C.

Edgar traveled alone. Because he was a minor Mexicana de Aviacion sat him in first class. The combination of flying by himself and leaving it all behind filled him with so much sadness that Edgar started to fight back the tears and gasped for air. He looked out the window: Mexico City glowed under the high noon sun. He wanted to see where Lumerso's house would be. He couldn't locate it. He closed the window curtain.

One of his uncle's drivers was waiting for him at the airport. Edgar arrived on an autumn afternoon, one of the first cold days in the city. The black Chrysler took the short route on the side road of Rock Creek Park, leading into Massachusetts Avenue, where most of the ambassadors lived.

When they got to the house, three maids were neatly lined up to receive him garden side. They took him inside, sat him at a table and served him chicken salad with celery, apples, and nuts. Edgar didn't enjoy the contrast in flavors. Gisela, the housekeeper, showed him his bedroom, and the library where he'd be taking English classes with Miss Charlotte. Edgar couldn't believe what his mother had done to him. Fortunately, he wouldn't be seeing her as often as his father. After Gisela showed him the bedroom with a view onto the gardens of the Vice President's residence, she spoke to him:

"The psychiatrist will be here too, twice a week; but if you want him every day, I can schedule it."

The word 'psychiatrist' pushed Edgar into a state of despair. He felt repulsion for himself, for Lumerso, for what they did together. He wondered if being gay was really a disease or a disgrace. He wanted to disappear, reincarnate in another body like in the comics.

Ms. Gisela had black hair and a white mole that divided the hair in two parts. Edgar stared at her until he finally thanked her for having been so kind to him.

"I like your hair very much," Edgar said with a shy smile.

He was mesmerized by the fact that he had a bathroom inside the room. He turned off the lights in the bedroom and was immediately hit by amazement as he saw through the bathroom window the perfectly illuminated Capitol Building and all the monuments. He realized right then that he did not remember the names he learned during past trips but thought to himself he better studied them again as this city was going to be his new home for a while.

However, life in the house on Massachusetts Avenue didn't last long. President Vicente Fox returned Uncle Guillermo to his country. Edgar's mother loathed the idea of seeing him back in Mexico City and, even worse, the probability of a reconciliation with Lumerso. So, before having to deal with any of that she decided that her son ought to stay in Washington, D.C. and enrolled him in a boarding school there. Edgar's expenses abroad wiped away the family's bank accounts, but Magdalena didn't mind eating canned tuna every day as long as her son remained far away from Lumerso and finished his professional studies in the United States.

Edgar started to get used to Washington, D.C. He loved how cosmopolitan and bohemian the city was. He had friends from different countries that he'd met at boarding school and during the year he lived with his uncle Guillermo. The dorms adjacent to the school allowed him certain freedom. He could arrive after ten o'clock at night and go out during the weekends without having to give any explanations.

During his senior year at high school he applied for scholarships at Georgetown University and George Mason University. Both accepted Edgar and aided him with full tuition and housing scholarships. Edgar was happy. He'd no longer have to depend financially on his parents. To make sure money would not be a problem, he took on a couple of jobs to cover the remaining expenses.

The visits with the psychiatrist, Dr. Morrison, helped him accept his own identity and helped him understand he was not a sick person, as his mother repeatedly had told him. He never spoke again of the topic with either of his parents. During Santiago's, his father, visits, the conversations about women started to vanish.

One night they went out for dinner before Santiago took a flight back to Mexico. During the years Edgar had spent in Washington, D.C. they managed to become much closer. They enjoyed what they never did together in Mexico City. They got together to play squash, run, lift weights. Edgar also took him several times to the zoo during the summer. Seeing a couple of pandas devour a kilo of bamboo in seconds was something they both enjoyed.

"You know? I have no problem with you being gay," his father said one time, apologizing in the middle of dessert. Santiago's eyes teared up. A smile lit up Edgar's face. Santiago patted his cheek like he used to do all the time when his son was a child.

That night, after putting his dad on a cab, Edgar decided to walk home. The night was freezing. Edgar lived a few blocks away from the Capitol. He looked up and saw a radiant moon close to a dazzling Venus. He sat a while to contemplate the dome of the Capitol. He thought of how fortunate he was for having lived in such a beautiful city. Now he'd like to return to Mexico, to work in his father's pharmaceutical company.

A tall guy in a long coat asked him for a cigarette. The man was so bundled up that Edgar could only see pink cheeks in the stranger's face. The street was desolate. Only a few cars drove down Pennsylvania Avenue. Edgar replied that he didn't smoke, but a cigarette in such cold weather would be great. They started to walk and stopped at a gay bar on the next corner. A video of Madonna dressed in camo was playing, she was singing *American Life*. A man was enjoying a beer while imitating her moves. Aside from that, the place was empty. The bartender was glad to see them. Edgar asked for a Cosmopolitan and a pack of cigarettes.

"I'm John and I want one of those too," the stranger chimed in.

John was born in the state of Connecticut. His parents were already old people when he came to the world. He had the chance to live with them for a short time until they died when he was twenty. Edgar felt sadness when John told him that, but then he added that he was happy for having known them, that his life had been extraordinary so far. They kept talking for a couple of hours until at two in the morning the place closed. Edgar was still happy for the acceptance he had finally gotten from his father. Without knowing why, he took a chance and impulsively kissed John.

"Is that the alcohol talking?" John asked confused.

"I think so," Edgar answered in between giggles.

They went looking for a taxi. Only one came by but didn't stop. It was past two in the morning. The subway only worked until midnight. They had no other way to get home but walking. John mentioned that when the night was that quiet and there were no taxis it was because it was about to snow. Edgar found his words funny. Everything seemed funny to him. The alcohol made him like that.

"I'm ten and a half blocks from my place," Edgar finally said, putting his gloves and hat on. John tied the scarf around his neck.

"But just one and a half from mine," John replied in a competitive tone.

They walked vigorously until they made it to the small alley at Duncan Place, where John lived with three roommates. They tried not to make noise, but the drinks had gone to Edgar's head. When they climbed the stairs of the old townhouse, the oysters he ate with his father covered the first steps. John held him by his back and pulled him to the bedroom. He sat him on an armchair and closed the door. Then he returned to clean the stairs. That's when he found his two roommates inspecting what had happened. The two liked that John had finally brought someone home.

When Edgar woke up the next morning the first thing he saw were John's blue eyes contemplating him.

"You want me to go and never come back?" Edgar asked with his impeccable English.

John didn't answer. He looked him in the eyes. It'd seemed like he'd fallen in love with this beautiful Mexican man.

John was finishing an internship for a Connecticut Senator in the Capitol. The following month he'd be stable in a new position. Besides, with the inheritance from his parents he'd bought a townhouse in P St. in Dupont Circle. John was happy to date Edgar. One afternoon, after going to the gym, they went for dinner to Burrito Brothers. It was a place they both enjoyed during the week. John put inside the burrito a ring he found in a cereal box. It was an aluminum ring with a red glass stone. John thought

Edgar would love it. After a third bite, the ring fell on the plate. John stood. He went down on one knee and asked him to move in together. Edgar's face changed colors. He'd enjoyed his time with John but moving in with him changed all his plans. Edgar saw his expression of happiness. The frozen smile he kept on his face, waiting for his answer. The man seated next to them also waited impatiently the end of the scene before filling his next burrito. Edgar saw him and replied almost without thinking:

"Of course, yes."

He knew that in a couple of months he was going back to Mexico to work with his father. How was he going to tell John that he was planning on returning to his country? He didn't. Instead, Edgar kissed him tenderly on the lips. John hugged him saying he was everything to him, that they were going to be happy for the rest of their lives. Edgar thought immediately of Lumerso and wondered what might have become of his life.

Upon returning home he did what he'd done endless times. He googled his old friend to see if he could find him somewhere on the Internet. But Edgar didn't find him. The name Lumerso De la Torre didn't show up anywhere.

Chapter XIX

Roma Neighborhood, 1987

Josefina was happy she met Ignacio as a young adult starting a new chapter in her life. The two had a lot of things in common, they both especially wanted to travel the whole world and see every corner of it. They truly hated the idea of staying for too long in the chaotic place that Mexico City had become. They were young, all of life's experiences were there for the taking. Ignacio had just abandoned Law School at UNAM, it wasn't for him. Numbers were more his thing. And he also understood that combining his knowledge of the law with his passion for numbers was the best way for him to make good money. He didn't want to go into sales like his father did. Josefina continued studying nursing with the simple goal of just having a degree. She didn't want to become another of so many housewives, as there was an overabundance of them in

Mexico. She was different, she had such big dreams! She refused to live locked up, much less, tied down to the responsibilities of a home.

One Saturday they went to the movies to see *"Fatal Attraction."* Josefina didn't understand why they told such vicious story when it could have been a romantic movie without the need to show that much violent behavior. Ignacio truly appreciated her speaking up about how she felt, even if they were talking about fictional characters.

After leaving the theater, they walked until they made it to the Cibeles Fountain. Josefina sat quietly, enjoying the ever-changing movements of the water. The dancing lights lit up her young face. The water kept splashing her, causing her to yelp and giggle. Ignacio pulled out a handkerchief and dried her face.

"I'm pregnant..." Josefina said after a silent moment, anxious and fearful.

The news froze him with fear. Their plans were about to vanish. The first thing that crossed Ignacio's mind was that they shouldn't have a child right away. They didn't have a house, not a cent to his name, much less any means or income to take care of a child.

Josefina became upset when she saw that his reaction wasn't the answer she expected or hoped for. She was three months pregnant. Getting an abortion would be the last thing she would ever do.

She went back home alone. Ignacio couldn't walk with her, he couldn't even shake the fear off his face.

They didn't talk for two weeks until Ignacio reappeared one morning with *mariachis* to ask her to marry him. He had reached an agreement with his father. If he began paying for the house he had in Condesa then it would be his when he turned thirty years old. Josefina's mother already knew about the pregnancy, so she too went out that day to celebrate her daughter's engagement.

Six months later Julieta was born.

They began to furnish the house with some furniture Victoria gave them when she sold her apartment before leaving for Toronto. It was enough to equip the first floor of the house. Josefina began working as a nurse in the State Hospital of Mexico and soon discovered that pretty much everything she saw there caused her light-headedness. Ignacio took a job in a law firm downtown, he actually liked that they both were pitching in to pay the bills. On top of that, Josefina's mother gave them a little money so they could begin their lives. During the nights Ignacio studied accounting. They weren't doing bad. They decided that Josefina didn't need to go back to work. When Julieta was just beginning to talk Josefina surprised Ignacio with the news that she was pregnant again. This time, Ignacio received the news better, perhaps even happier than before.

They started house renovations that began by fixing the humidity problems; later, they changed the doors and did a complete makeover of the kitchen and the bathrooms. Their house in Condesa became one of the best on the block.

In a few years Ignacio decided to leave his job at the firm to begin working independently as an accountant for several companies. Josefina devoted all her time to their home, but with a house with four bedrooms and two children, she needed help.

Six years after Julieta was born, they threw a party to celebrate Lumerso's third birthday. Ignacio wanted a big party for the boy of the family. That day they met Jimena, a pleasant young woman from Oaxaca who'd come to take care of some children. Josefina spent the afternoon asking her questions until, as the party came to an end, Jimena had a new job. Two days later she began working with the De la Torre family.

When Josefina realized she could give Jimena any task, from the favorite dishes, the ones Ignacio liked, to how he wanted the lines on his pants, she started to detach herself more and more from the household chores. In occasions she thought of her mother and how she'd never spoken to her again. Every so often she'd get postcards from a new country with a new phone number. Josefina threw away Victoria's mail for her. She felt jealousy that her mother kept traveling when she could barely handle a family. Amid the profound depressions everything overwhelmed and annoyed her. The small responsibilities from the house tormented her. She decided to talk to Ignacio about sending Lumerso and Julieta to study to another country or some boarding school; it didn't matter if it was in Mexico or anywhere else. She explained to her husband that it would be with the assumption that if they have a better education they'd be better candidates for future marriages. Ignacio listened to her; it didn't seem like such a bad idea to him. However, he thought it'd be better for Julieta to go once she finished elementary school. She was too young at that moment. Lumerso could stay in the city and do just fine; after all, he was a guy like him, Ignacio explained.

In between the fights with Ignacio, Josefina began going to a psychologist. She lived in depression. Didn't enjoy the comfortable life she had. Ignacio worked at home. Josefina couldn't stand seeing him all day sitting in the bedroom that had become his office. Josefina no longer gave instructions to Jimena, who seemed to make all the decisions at home. She spent most of her time holed up in her room. The severe changes in her personality kept her even further away from the children and from Ignacio. Julieta rarely ever talked to her. She was afraid of her own mother, never found her in a good mood. Lumerso was something else. He'd go into the room without knocking. Would tell her about what he'd done during the day, though he knew his mother didn't listen. He asked her questions about what he'd just told her, but Josefina didn't know how to answer him.

After Julieta's trip to Europe and the return of her mother, Victoria, Josefina started to feel full of life and joy. The therapies seemed to have worked. She listened to her mother when she told her about everything she had done and experienced during her long absence. She went back to helping prepare meals alongside Jimena and took better care of Ignacio. He was happy that his wife had returned to life.

When her mother Victoria died, Josefina returned to isolating herself in her room. She couldn't believe that her mother would come back only to die. She began to take pills once again for depression, this time along with glasses of wine, until Ignacio discovered what she was doing. After that, he said alcohol was forbidden in the house and made sure Josefina did not have any temptations.

A few months after the death of Victoria, Josefina still wouldn't come out of her bedroom. Neither did Lumerso. Ignacio was beginning to think that the family was going crazy. One afternoon he found his wife in the bedroom, lying on the floor, in her pajamas. He could tell she was sedated with medication and decided not to wake her up but, instead, take care of the core problem.

A week later, Josefina found herself in a rehabilitation center in Ajusco. She spent a month there. When she returned home, she was a changed woman. She listened to Lumerso's stories and replied coherently to his questions. Jimena complained that she had more work than ever. Ignacio was happy for having recovered his family once more. The bank accounts were something else. Every time he looked at them, he realized that the money in there was depleting faster than he'd like to see. He wanted to pull Julieta from the Swiss boarding-school. He thought that if Lumerso was capable of getting over his desire to run away and Josefina was able to deal with her depression, Julieta could adapt once again to Mexico City too. That's why when Julieta out of the blue told her father that she didn't want to continue studying in Switzerland, Ignacio accepted her demands without much resistance. Julieta never found out about the economic difficulties her father faced during that time until it was too late to change any of it.

A year after reuniting with her family under the same roof, Josefina waited for Ignacio in the kitchen to serve him his dinner. Jimena had gone home already. Julieta was in her bedroom. Lumerso was still going to the university finishing a model for a new project.

Ignacio came back home that night with a bottle of red wine. He poured a small amount for Josefina. He poured himself a big glass. He delved into the chicken breast with tomato salad. He poured himself another glass. He told Josefina that the chicken was a bit salty and next time she shouldn't use salt, like the cardiologist recommended. Josefina tried the chicken but found it didn't have any taste. Jimena hadn't used any salt. Ignacio took another sip of wine and almost immediately the glass fell alongside him to the floor. Josefina tried to get him up. She loosened the knot of his tie. She saw that Ignacio's face was getting horribly pale. Julieta, from her bedroom and in between the music, heard her mother's screams. She ran down the stairs. She tried to remember the first-aid class, but her father was already dead. A devastating heart-attack killed him. Josefina wept and screamed until Julieta gave her some pills she found in her father's nightstand to help her calm down.

Half an hour later, Ignacio De la Torre's body was *en route* to the morgue.

Josefina stayed in a drugged-up state from then on. She didn't learn that Lumerso was in the hospital too nor that Julieta had returned home after the funeral. She was in no condition to understand why they had to move to an apartment, or the reason why they abandoned the house at Condesa. Her thoughts had neither continuity nor coherency. She remembered her mother and father fighting in the kitchen of the apartment in the Roma neighborhood. Called names that none of them ever heard her say before. Jimena lost her job and when her son Arturo went to the house in Condesa looking for any kind of remuneration for his mother all he found were signs that read: *"Seized."* He never again returned. When he went back to the Buenos Aires neighborhood, he told his mother that the rich people were no longer rich.

Upon moving to the apartment in Romita Josefina stopped talking. She took plenty of medications without having any understanding of what they would do to her. Julieta continued with her job as secretary in a government office. Since Julieta and Lumerso went to work during the day no one took care of Josefina for extended periods of time. When they'd returned home, the children would make various attempts to take care of their mother. Julieta would try to feed her, but Josefina wouldn't swallow more than a few bites. Lumerso would insist that at least she should drink some juice or a shake but always had a hard time managing to convince her. He talked to her like he did as a child with Grandma Victoria. Josefina could see Lumerso's lips move but didn't comprehend what he was trying to tell her.

Every morning Julieta opened the balcony door to let some fresh air in for her mother and later Lumerso would seat her in front of the TV, but Josefina didn't care if it was on or off. After she left for work, Julieta always sent Lumerso text messages so he wouldn't forget to close the balcony door before going out.

Lumerso began working as a masseur after the experiences with Genaro. He would work on three to five clients daily. Many times, he could barely cope with the large amount of erotic massages people requested in the city. Sometimes it seemed to him as if he were the only masseuse in town. A great deal of time was spent traveling. So his mind was on *What subway line must I take?* Or *Where do I need to go for the next massage?* Or *In which metro station do I need to get off?* On top of that, he was always wondering what kind of psychopath he might find that day. But then he would tell himself that that was the least of his troubles, in the end they were all looking for the same thing: a caress, a penetration, or a hand job.

The day of the accident Julieta left a banana milkshake for her mother and left in a hurry. She had an interview for a better post in the delegation. She woke Lumerso so he'd feed their mother. Lumerso had arrived at four in the morning. He was so wasted, he didn't even remember where he lived. He ignored Julieta's calls. Kept sleeping throughout the morning. He was awakened by some grumbling and a loud noise on the street. Before looking out the window, he went to the bathroom. He peeked into the TV room but didn't see his mother anywhere. While taking his time peeing, he once again heard whispering coming from downstairs. He called his mother a couple of times. Found the armchair full of excrement and piss. He looked at the clock. It was past noon.

He went out to the balcony to see what was going on. Saw the body of his mother lying on the sidewalk. He rushed down from the fourth floor to the step where his mother had fallen. Lumerso hugged her, shaking her body while he cried and wept like a child begging for her to wake up. His weeping and screams were so desperate they bounced through the whole block. The sound of the ambulance could be heard above him. He felt the cellphone vibrate in the pocket of his pants. He had twenty missed calls from Julieta.

Chapter XX

Condesa Neighborhood, 2019

Edgar hadn't seen Lumerso since the day he found him at the steam bath. He couldn't believe that nine years had passed. Lumerso had just had a massage in the area when he decided to enter the supermarket in Condesa to buy some aromatic oils. While passing by the cosmetics area he recognized the perfect profile of Edgar. He looked more handsome than ever. The years had turned him into a dashing man with eyes full of wisdom. Lumerso wanted to go unnoticed. When he heard Edgar's voice calling out to him, Lumerso didn't know what to say. He was sleep-deprived and so very tired. He felt as if he hadn't slept in a decade. A long beard covered part of his face. He was wearing skinny jeans, a white t-shirt and a sweatshirt tied around his waist. The June showers had begun. A wave of freezing air was hitting the city.

Edgar asked him if he was alright. Lumerso answered that he was working a lot and that sometimes he even forgot to eat, but that he was resting that night at least. Edgar restrained himself from asking what kind of work he was doing. Once, after looking long and hard for him, he discovered his picture, with another name, in the *Grindr* app. In the description they talked about erotic massages of any kind for passive and active individuals. Edgar wanted to find out more, but it pained him to find him there. He got out of the app as quickly as he could.

They continued talking about the last encounter they had when they were thrown in jail. Edgar said that they should go out again, like in the old days. Lumerso didn't know what to answer. The old days were during their childhood. He thought about the number of men that had used his body since then. From the person Edgar knew to the man he'd become there was nothing left. He replied that it was better that they hang out some other time, when he wasn't so busy.

"I want to take you out on a date," Edgar said in a loving tone.

Edgar looked good. He was dressed in a three-piece pinstripe blue suit with a white button up with cufflinks and no tie. His hair was long, combed back. He'd just returned from Miami, so he was tanned, and that glow perfectly highlighted his amazing green eyes. It was so hard to say no to him.

Lumerso kept walking and Edgar followed him like a shadow. He couldn't find the oils. He walked to the pharmacy area. He was going nuts trying to get rid of Edgar. He didn't want to be with him. Edgar was a worldly person, successful, handsome. How could they've spent so much time growing up together and now be so different?

They stepped out to Michoacan Avenue. Edgar insisted that he'd follow him until he agreed to going out with him. Lumerso replied that he was hungry, so he proposed they go to dinner immediately and that would be their date. Edgar wasn't expecting that answer. He had two bags with eggs, milk, cereal, and bread. He wanted to leave them in the car but imagined that if he went to leave them there Lumerso would bail on him. He found himself replying that he loved the idea. An opportunity like that probably wouldn't present itself for another nine years, he said jokingly.

They walked down one block until Edgar stopped at an Italian restaurant. They sat inside but close to the garden. The waiter let them chat. He came once in a while to see if they needed more wine or water. They ate some Fettucine Alfredo with a side of chicken piccata deviled style. Edgar insisted on paying the bill. Lumerso pulled out of his pocket a small plastic bag with hundred, two hundred and five hundred bills. Edgar didn't know what to say. Each of them paid their part.

The sun had set. A drizzle was falling, making everything on the street wet. Edgar explained that he'd left the car in the supermarket parking lot. The two hid underneath Edgar's suit-jacket and they ran. Upon climbing into the car, Edgar took his hand and kissed it. He told him he was the love of his life and asked Lumerso to forgive him for everything, that they could perhaps start from scratch right then and there. Lumerso spoke with nothing but his eyes. He wanted to tell him that he was no longer that boy he knew.

Edgar grabbed him by the neck to kiss him on the lips when a knock on the window interrupted him:

"You're taking off?" the guard asked.

Edgar began driving. Traffic was heavy, a line of lights hidden amid the storm that was beginning to get aggressive. Edgar drove with only one hand, with the other he touched Lumerso's leg. He left him before the old building in Romita.

"You live alone?" Edgar asked.

Lumerso told him that he lived with his sister Julieta and that his mother had died. Edgar hugged him telling that, that wasn't a proper date and that he'd be picking him up on Saturday at three in the afternoon.

"How should I dress?" Lumerso asked, finally smiling shyly.

"Like that, like the Lumerso De la Torre that I knew," Edgar said, showing his perfect teeth.

When Lumerso got home he felt different. He forgot for a few hours that he was prostituting himself for a living. That the massages were simply an excuse to cover up what he really was.

The apartment was all dirty, everything had aged in a short time. No one cleaned up anymore. Julieta returned home from work to lock herself up in her room. Her weight kept going up. She had premature white hairs but refused to dye her hair. She and Lumerso didn't talk to each other. The dishes piled up in the sink and part of the kitchen table. Everything changed since Josefina's death. Julieta blamed Lumerso for not having closed the door, and he her for not committing their mother to a psychiatric hospital. Lumerso himself didn't understand for what he worked so much for. He handed most of the money to Julieta, but she perhaps hid it underneath the mattress. She didn't buy anything. Every so often some food would appear in the fridge. It seemed as if Julieta never ate, though her appearance would argue otherwise.

On Saturday, the day of the date, at ten minutes to three in the afternoon Lumerso was waiting for Edgar sitting on one of the benches in a park in Romita. He was impatient. He'd shaved off the beard. Bought a pair of white jeans and a red checkered button up shirt. He hadn't had sex in the last couple of days. He thought of the possibilities of doing it with Edgar. He was sure that he was aware of what he did for a living; otherwise he'd have asked that day, when he had the chance to do it. He, on the other hand, knew beforehand that Edgar was working at his father's pharmaceutical business.

Lumerso had gel in his hair, he looked like the person he was before the death of his father. He looked at the time on his cellphone, it was three on the dot. Seconds later, Edgar arrived in his BMW. After parking, he got out of the car and gave Lumerso a bear hug along with a couple of pats in the back. Lumerso didn't remember the last time someone embraced him with so much affection. Immediately, Edgar invited him into his car, he opened the door for him like the gentleman he was.

As they drove jazz music played softly on the radio. Lumerso wanted to hold his hand like he did before but decided not to. He thought of the times he was in cars with strangers and they all immediately wanted to put their hand down his pants or hold his hand as if they had been boyfriends their whole lives. Edgar was nervous, Lumerso never saw him like that, but he could tell he was anxious about something, this date perhaps. He was wearing a polo shirt that showed off his muscled arms and pectorals, gray dress pants and brown moccasins. He smelled of the same fragrance that he used as a teenager.

Edgar drove them to Camino Royal in Polanco. They parked and walked a few blocks until they got to a place they both liked: Asia Grill. They sat at the bar to have an appetizer. But when the hostess came by to take them to their table they decided to stay where they were and order from there. They liked the privacy and not having the other tables so close together.

Edgar talked about how well he was doing at his father's company, how he already bought an apartment in Santa Fe, where he lived during the week to be close to the Toluca airport, where the majority of the flights to the United States departed from. He also told him that Magdalena, his mother, had died the year before. While Santiago, his father, kept traveling every so often, but was dedicated to raising a pack of dogs that now lived at his place. He slept at his father's house on the weekends to keep him company. As Lumerso listened to him, he didn't know if he envied Edgar's life, or admired him for achieving everything he wished since childhood. He, however, was a whole other story, was responsible for all the bad choices he'd made. After drinking a glass of water after the half bottle of white wine, Edgar apologized to him:

"I'm incredibly nervous. Forgive me, please, for having abandoned you, and now I haven't stopped talking and… I don't know what to say, how have you been?"

Lumerso was quick to dodge the question and said they should better order something to eat;

otherwise they'd be picking the both of them off the floor. There was a pause as he considered what to say before finally telling him that everything in his life was the same. That nothing he'd planned had worked out, that the death of his father ruined everything, that they lost their belongings because the bank accounts were empty before his father died. That he couldn't finish his degree, that his mother died in a horrible accident and Julieta suffered from depression just like his mother. That was his life. One tragedy after another. Edgar didn't know how to reply to that.

When they finished having some sauteed shrimp covered in sweet-and-sour sauce with coconut, Edgar proposed a walk. He said that they ought to do like the Buddhists advise: live in the now. Forget all that happened in the past and enjoy the current moment. They were there together in that moment and it now belonged to them.

Lumerso approved of the idea. They left the restaurant and walked for a while until making it to Reforma Avenue. They stopped to watch an exhibition of images from the Mexican Golden Cinema. It was past six in the afternoon when they entered the *Zona Rosa*. They had some margaritas in a bar to a side of Londres Street, Lumerso kissed Edgar in the lips. They were happy. They held hands like two teenagers. They kept walking until they made it to the Glorieta de los Insurgentes. Once there they found an improvised center for the testing of STDs, VDs and HIV.

"Why don't we go in?" Edgar asked spontaneously.

The question froze Lumerso. He'd never gotten one of those tests, only taken antibiotics for venereal diseases. He didn't even remember the names anymore. Lumerso insisted that they live in the present and reminded Edgar that thinking about horrible diseases was a thing of the past. Edgar replied that doing the test in the present would help them into the future they'd build together.

Edgar went in first. Lumerso waited outside for a while until he decided to catch up to him. His face was very pale. A woman dressed in black explained to them what they should do in case of having a positive test: they had to follow treatments and contact all the people with whom they've had sex without protection. Lumerso thought that his list would be much larger than all the people walking by Glorieta de los Insurgentes in that moment. His hands were shaking, he felt restless. His mouth was dry. The drinks, the strange food and Edgar's insistence in doing the testing made the joyful moment that they were enjoying a few minutes ago disappear.

After what felt like days waiting, the counselor asked them if they wanted the news together or individually. The woman seemed so unemotional as she spoke. She was terribly calm and her glasses slipped down constantly. She couldn't be more than thirty years old. With a tremor in his voice Lumerso replied that he rather heard the news by himself. Edgar stopped him by saying they should get the news together. The woman shrugged and called them behind a black curtain, which she closed, leaving on the other side one person whose life she'd also changed forever, it was a red-haired teenage boy who cried while hugging a box full of condoms.

"We've detected the HIV virus in both of you. Are you a couple?" she asked.

Edgar's face turned every color. He wanted to run away, deal a blow to the woman, or to Lumerso. He opened the curtain and looked outside.

"This is for you," the woman said, handing him the printed results.

Lumerso thought it was all the same if he had it on a piece of paper or not. Edgar sat down; he couldn't articulate in his mind what the woman had just said. Lumerso grabbed him by the arm. Edgar immediately took his hand off him. The philosophy of living the moment had led him to receiving the worst news of his existence. Lumerso tried to hug him again until Edgar yelled:

"It was you, fucking asshole."

Lumerso didn't know what to say, the woman tried to calm them. Edgar ran out. Lumerso followed him.

"Leave me alone, fucking shit. My mother was right," Edgar said before taking off running.

Edgar's words saddened him in that instant more than ever. Lumerso didn't know what direction to take. He could feel the looks of everyone on him. The consultant called him, she gave him a bag of condoms and a list of clinics that would support him in this first stage. Lumerso took them. He couldn't think right. He walked without thinking where was he going. He didn't know what the worst news were: that Edgar was infected just like him… or that he too was positive.

He walked down Oaxaca Avenue trying to get back home. He walked by the office of Dr. Vargas, the psychiatrist. Rang the bell several times, but no one answered. Then he phoned him but got no answer either. Then he called Edgar, to the number he had just given him. The call went straight to voicemail. He decided to write him a text message:

"I don't know why these things happen to me with the people I love. You don't know how sorry I am."

Lumerso remembered the afternoon of his father's funeral, when he made love to Edgar for the one and only time. It was impossible that it was him who gave Edgar HIV. It had been nine years since that afternoon. When Dr. Vargas answered his call Lumerso didn't know what to say to him anymore. He hadn't gotten home yet. He told him that he was walking down Oaxaca Avenue and wanted to say hi, nothing to be alarmed about, that everything was wonderful, better than ever, that life had given him more than he ever asked for. Before hanging up the phone Dr. Vargas exclaimed:

"You know that I know you're lying!"

Lumerso didn't want to reply. He just disconnected the call and blocked the number.

Chapter XXI

Romita, 2019

Lumerso walked back to the apartment. He was sweating. The red checkered button up was soaked in sweat. He opened the door and was surprised to find everything clean and organized. He thought that finally Julieta had given a good use to his money, that she'd hired someone to do the cleaning. He heard noises in the entrance bathroom.

"Julieta, are you there?" Lumerso asked.

"It's me, Jimena," an unrecognizable voice answered.

Lumerso was happy to see her, but didn't know how to express it. Jimena explained that Julieta had asked her to come over so she could give her the severance pay she'd been waiting to get for so many years. She sent her the key to the apartment with Gustavo, Jimena's son. When she came earlier, she saw the apartment was a mess and began cleaning. Suddenly Jimena stopped and pointed out that she was in no condition to continue doing it. The pain in her waist didn't let her move like before, and on top of that, her diabetes was killing her. She was grateful for the money; it was a lot more than she expected. She was going to use it for the grandchildren that were about to start high school. Lumerso was listening to her. He pulled out a tequila bottle and told her to sit beside him for a while to talk. Invited her to have a drink. Jimena declined. She went to fetch her purse.

"This is yours… I'm sorry for not having given it to you before, but I didn't know how to…" Jimena said as she gave him a notebook while opening the apartment door.

Lumerso took the green notebook in his hands, pressed it to his face like a long-lost lover and took a long whiff of its musty smell. The color had aged, his name had faded from the cover. He remembered how much he missed it. Realized that his handwriting wasn't as good as before. He wanted to catch up to Jimena to hug her, kiss her, thank her, but he was no longer the Lumerso she knew. Lumerso looked out the balcony until he saw her disappearing as she went across a long street crossing diagonal to his building. He noticed for the first time that one of her legs was longer than the other. He was confused, in between the news he'd just been given, Edgar, Jimena, Dr. Vargas, and the return of his journal, he felt fragile, vulnerable; wanted to cry like a child in his mother's arms. He stretched out on the couch and looked up the last entry he wrote about Edgar:

"Condesa, October 9th, 2002

It's not easy to write this day. I may never do it again. Edgar has left to never come back. It hurts inside here and everywhere. I don't even know where it hurts. I cannot swallow. It's as if a gigantic knot won't even let me breathe. I want to die. I feel so embarrassed for what I did to him in Chapultepec, but I know he wanted it too; if not, he wouldn't have let it happen, right? I will never see him again. His mother hates me. I went to his house looking for him and she didn't let me in. Surely Edgar left me a letter or a message. What am I gonna do without him? Maybe I'll go love crazy? People go crazy or suicidal, like Romeo and Juliet. I have no more friends and Edgar was the only one who knew I'm gay. I don't want to be like this anymore. Tomorrow I'd like to wake up and marry Claudia like he wanted to. I hope he'll love me and not forget me and come back for me. I have no motive to write in you anymore. What am I gonna write? That my dad hates me for being gay and that my mom gets depressed without reason all the time. Well diary, goodbye for now; if you happen to see Edgar tell him I love him, I love him, and then I love him more."

Lumerso closed the notebook, thought of the man Edgar had become. He was a worldly person, educated and polyglot. He stood to see himself in the mirror Jimena had just cleaned up. He felt shame as he explored his face. It was swollen, yellowish; he was an immoral man full of falsehoods and, the worst of all, a sex worker. Edgar was right. He continued being a bad influence. He threw himself onto the couch to think about what he was going to do with the short time he had left to live. Thought of living it to the maximum, probably keep giving massages. After all, it was the best he could do. He didn't know the techniques, but the men just wanted a younger man to touch and caress them until he made them ejaculate. He opened the *Grindr* app on the cellphone. He had three requests. It was already past ten at night. He closed his eyes and hugged his notebook making sure it wouldn't escape again.

In his dreams he saw Edgar in a white suit entering a glass church in the middle of the woods. White petals adorned the hallway. A heavy rain fell mercilessly everywhere. He was waiting for him in a cream-colored suit at the altar. Lightning left the church in darkness. Ignacio, Josefina, Julieta and her husband, Dr. Vargas, were all seated on the first row. Behind them were all the men Lumerso had slept with. He recognized Antonio, Enrique, Genaro, Gabriel, Garzo and the rest of them. They had big teeth and their penises were outside their clothes and starting to get hard. Jimena was the priestess. Edgar was wearing a pink veil covering his face.

"You can kiss the bride," Jimena was saying.

"But he's a groom," Lumerso was responding.

Jimena wasn't paying attention and waited for them to kiss.

The banging of a door woke him up. Julieta had entered. She didn't notice any difference in the apartment. Only saw the keys Jimena had left on the table.

"It was a good thing... What you did with the money I mean," Lumerso said.

Julieta made a face and looked for some water to drink.

"Look what I've got," Lumerso said with enthusiasm showing her the journal.

Julieta asked him coldly what it was. Lumerso replied that it was his old diary and that Jimena finally brought it back to him. Julieta grabbed it without any interest. She looked at it on both sides and gave it back. She locked herself in her room. Lumerso didn't know what else to add.

Lumerso continued working as if nothing had changed in his life. Sometimes he would think about getting in touch with Edgar, but then remembered that he was the one who had blocked him out of his life in every possible way. He kept busy offering massage services. He kept going between Las Lomas, Roma and Condesa. Those were the neighborhoods he frequented the most. One night he received a text message from a client who wanted a massage in a prestigious hotel on Reforma Avenue: the St. Vincent. He only knew it from the outside. He scheduled the appointment like any other. The man requested that he came dressed-up so nobody would question if he belonged there or ask him to leave. He did as he was told and had no problems.

Lumerso crossed the hotel lobby and took the elevator. He arrived at the suite on the sixth floor. He rang the doorbell and a bald man opened the door. Lumerso noticed that he was wearing a hotel bathrobe; he told him to lie face down on the bed and get comfortable while he washed his hands before they got started. Upon returning to the bedroom area he found the man face up and with two more men lying beside him; one was darker and the other white, fat, and hairy. They were all Spaniards. The men were naked and began touching each other.

"I'm sorry, we agreed that it was only one person. If it's going to be like this, you better call someone else," Lumerso said as he turned around, heading for the door.

The bald one replied that he should calm down, that he wouldn't have to work. They just want him to lie down and they'd give him the massage.

Lumerso felt nauseated when he saw them together on the bed. They reminded him of vultures hungry for fresh meat. He thought of everything he had suffered in life because of men like the ones there… He vomited in his mouth thinking of Genaro, Enrique in Cuernavaca, La Casona… and the list seemed endless. He felt filled with rage, grudge, hate and a thirst for vengeance.

After reaching an agreement, he explained that it would be preferable to practice safe sex, since it'd be better for everyone. His mind, however, was thinking about something else. He'd be the weapon for these fuckers that wanted to take advantage of him once more. He wanted to take vengeance on all those who had ruined his life. The men said that they were all healthy and clean. They even claimed they did not have any kind of venereal diseases. But then they said that if all of them were healthy, then it would be okay to fuck without condoms and enjoy themselves to the fullest. Lumerso pretended to leave. One of them grabbed him by the arm so he wouldn't. He served him vodka. Told him to have a drink. They diluted the Viagra pill in the drink. They sat for a while. Lumerso hated being in that luxurious place. He saw through the window the fountain of Diana in front, thought of how he'd like it if the Huntress aimed her arrow at him and at everyone there.

After another half an hour drinking more and more, popping pills, and smoking a bit of marijuana, the three men undressed Lumerso and took him to bed. One of them insisted in between chuckles that without condom the fucking was a lot more pleasurable, that they could enjoy it fully; after all, they were all very healthy. The men kept laughing; especially the bald one, he was in heaven. They started what looked like a Greek-Roman orgy. One on top of Lumerso, another inside him and the other in the mouth. After an hour they all had released their semen a couple of times. Lumerso left them on the bed and went to the bathroom. The fat one followed him. He handed him the promised two thousand pesos.

"Can I take a shower?" Lumerso asked.

The bald one answered yes without any enthusiasm. Lumerso took his time in the bathroom. After he showered, he put on some perfume and a touch of gel. He lifted everything he found there and put it in his pockets. He then realized they'd just blocked his profile in *Grindr* where he offered massage services. He didn't care. He opened the door. Left without saying goodbye. When he was in the hallway he ran for the elevator.

The bald one went into the bathroom. He needed glasses to see. Apparently, the fag had left a note.

"You've all been infected with HIV."

"Son of a bitch!" the bald one yelled.

He rushed to the door but Lumerso was already on a taxi on the way home. That was his revenge. He got even with three people for everything everyone had done to him throughout his life. With his vengeance he made sure that the chain of pleasure-pain-torture-revenge would go on and on. He didn't even recognize himself. Seeking a life, he found one misfortune after another. He was sure that he hadn't infected Edgar. Hated himself for what he'd just done, but regret wouldn't get him anywhere.

He sat on a bench in front of his building. Didn't want to go into the apartment. Didn't want to listen to Julieta snore in her bedroom while he lay wide awake bored and tired. It was one in the morning. He went to a place he knew on Insurgentes Avenue. It was Sunday, so the place was packed with men. He felt liberated. He was no longer afraid of life, or anyone. He could sleep with whomever he wanted and also with those he didn't want too but did for money. He was an official carrier of the virus, like the card they gave him at the clinic said.

The bar was dark. Alejandra Guzman pulsated at top volume through the speakers. He took the stairs leading to a third bar on the higher level. Lumerso drank a couple of vodkas before getting to the end of the hallway. He couldn't see. He felt as if tentacles manhandled him. Lumerso shooed them away like wild flies. He got to where a crowd enjoyed other bodies with lust. He didn't want to participate. The heat overwhelmed him. One couldn't breathe in that place. He removed his shirt and trousers but let someone else tear away his underwear. He hugged the clothes with his right hand. He was naked. Only wearing his sneakers with pink socks. He sensed many mouths kissing and sucking his penis until he felt it enter someone's ass hole. Lumerso didn't enjoy it. He let them do all kinds of stuff until they ejaculated. Stayed there until dawn when they were beginning to empty the establishment. In his arms he still held his clothes.

Chapter XXII

Lausanne, 2003

Julieta looked nervous. They were putting her on a plane to Switzerland without her consent. She was a young woman who could make her own decisions, or at least that's what she thought. She felt her stomach was in knots, she kept feeling the *arrachera tacos* Jimena prepared for breakfast trying to make a comeback through her esophagus, she felt extremely nauseated and ready to throw up at any moment.

Josefina, Ignacio and Lumerso walked with her all the way to the boarding gate. Ignacio maintained good relations with authorities at the airport which let him into all the restricted access areas. It was a pity that he didn't travel as much as he'd like.

Julieta looked into her mother's eyes in search of strength, but she just arranged her hair, telling her to talk to people only if they spoke to her first. Lumerso was the only one who cried. Josefina looked at Julieta as if she'd just gotten a weight off herself. She thought Lumerso didn't need as much attention as her. She was afraid that her daughter might become pregnant before her time in Mexico City. However, she thought that over there in Switzerland things were different. She'd be in the care of the school and any accident that may happen was their responsibility.

Ignacio hugged Julieta whispering into her ear how much he loved her. Julieta didn't want to let go. She held onto him as if she were about to be swept away into a dark unknowable ocean.

She had her hair pulled up into a neat and formal style. She wore a knee-length blue winter dress and white socks that covered her whole leg. A black beret, scarf, and red coat. That was how her mother had dressed her. It looked like a copy of the uniform of the new academy they chose as her boarding school abroad.

For all of her fifteen years Julieta had been a bit fat. Since she was a child, she fought with her weight. Being short didn't help either. Josefina put her in every single diet she came across. Nothing worked. The day of the trip, giant zits were beginning to pop out across her forehead. She was scared. She came to think that her mother was ashamed of her, and that was why she was sending her to study abroad. Her legs were shaking. The only time she got on a plane before was when they all went to Playa del Carmen. She remembered the crystalline ocean, the white sand, the starfishes she pulled out of the water and that Ignacio insisted that she return to the ocean. Julieta thought that they were the same that shone in the sky but had lost their way.

Lumerso was younger, that was why he didn't recall having been on a plane.

Julieta began to cry from the moment her father told her he loved her. Josefina stayed stone-faced the entire time. The Swiss Air agent approached, took her gently by the arm and helped her with the vanity case she had with her. The De la Torre family didn't wait until the plane took off. Ignacio had some new contracts to write and couldn't wait.

Lumerso felt sadness for Julieta; he could see in her face that she didn't want to leave. She liked living in the city; however, Josefina insisted that it was the best for a young lady like her. It was the only thing she could say. It pained Lumerso that they hadn't bought her a ticket back. Julieta had to stay in Switzerland until she finished her degree. Just thinking about it caused him even more rage.

The trip was a long one. Julieta had to sit beside a man who fell asleep on her shoulder. She didn't move. She thought it was her duty to hold up his monumental head. She waited until a flight attended walked by, so she'd see the imbecile she had over her. After a while she moved him, but moments later he returned to Julieta's shoulder. After eating a breakfast that consisted of an omelet with orange juice and fresh bread, Julieta could see the Alps that were beginning to be distinguishable through the clouds. She could feel just how far she was from home.

The stewardess helped her fill the immigration questionnaire before she got off the plane. Upon getting to the airport Julieta didn't know what to do or where to go to get the luggage. Instructions in different languages kept repeating the same thing through the loudspeakers. She had an advanced grasp of the English language and a little French, but she was so nervous her mind blocked her from interpreting anything into Spanish. She waited until the announcement came up in Italian. She thought she understood that language better.

A porter helped her with the luggage, he accompanied her to where she'd take the first train that would get her to the Central Station in Zurich. There she'd switch trains to the one heading to Lausanne. The trip was long, she needed to travel another three hours to get to the boarding school.

It was eleven in the morning and the train wouldn't depart until six minutes past three in the afternoon. Julieta waited. She wanted to see if they came to get her, like the instructions explained and her father had stated. She waited until noon. No one showed up. She began to feel fear. When she was about to go take a taxi, two slightly older girls showed up and called her by her full name. Julieta felt relief. She was hungry, but she didn't understand how much money she needed to exchange to buy something to eat. Vivian spoke to her in French and Cristina in Spanish. Vivian told her that they'd buy her something to eat inside the train. She continued her greeting telling her that they were sorry for the delay, but they'd missed the previous train. Besides, they imagined that the flight would be delayed, as it happens sometimes.

The trip on train was just as Julieta imagined it. The photographs they'd sent from the school were an exact copy of what she could marvel at on the way there. Forests surrounded by great lakes. Mountains of colors that she'd never seen and endless autumn shades. The trip, however, felt short to her. She confirmed that her French wasn't as bad as she thought. She and Vivian became fast friends during the trip. The three would share a dorm in the school. Cristina was a slim girl, tall and with wavy hair. She was dressed in the latest trends, not as conservative as Josefina had dressed Julieta. She told her about how happy she was to have gotten out of her house, since her parents couldn't understand her. By the time she'd finish school, she'd be eighteen already and then she could do with her life whatever she wanted. Julieta watched her in astonishment as she had a smoke after another. She flirted, opening her legs every time the ticket collector entered the compartment. In the middle of their chat she closed her eyes and fell asleep. Julieta wondered if she had narcolepsy or was simply as tired as her. Being so close to the mountains and feeling the first fresh winds of a season she didn't know changed Julieta's point of view of what her new life would be like.

They went to the admission's office as soon as they arrived at the school. It was a cabin built of cedar wood located in the middle of the campus, with gigantic, picturesque windows and a great fireplace in the lobby. There they were assigned their rooms and were given the schedule for orientation, which would start the next day at seven in the morning. Julieta said in English that she would like to speak with her family. The secretary, with a German accent, replied that there was no problem, that she'd already gotten in touch to tell them that Julieta had arrived at the boarding school. She added that on the weekend she'd be able to call them from the office for international students. Julieta didn't completely understand what the woman had just said but realized that she wouldn't be able to talk to them at that very moment.

Her new room was small but comfortable. A large window showed a blue lake surrounded by multi-colored trees and wild pines. To Julieta it seemed like the colors of autumn looked similar to the ones she'd learned in her art classes. Although those were shades created by nature itself. She wanted to remember that image forever. Underneath the window there was a bed and, on the other corner, near the bathroom door, the other two. They were separated by two nightstands. An old heater was placed in the middle of the other wall, followed by three desks with green lamps. Cristina removed her boots to continue sleeping. Vivian returned a few minutes later with a variety of cheeses, fruits, and crackers. They chatted sitting on the bed. The French one mentioned to Julieta that she'd chosen the best school in all of Switzerland. What she had to do was study, get good grades, and fate would do the rest. The good thing was that three universities took students directly from the school. Vivian was thinking about studying Chemical Engineering; likewise, she already had two universities fighting over her. Julieta didn't hear the last phrase. The flight and the time zone change had tired her too much. She collapsed on the mattress, her dinner still on the bed and inches away from her, until the alarm clock rang at half past six in the morning.

Julieta graduated from junior-high and high-school in Switzerland. During school breaks she traveled with Cristina to Madrid or spent the summer in France with Vivian. She didn't phone home frequently. Ignacio tried to call her at least twice a month. He sent the money orders to the school punctually. The two times he happened to be delayed, the school almost expelled Julieta back to Mexico. When Julieta found out that Lumerso had ran away from home she insisted on going back. It horrified her to think that her fragile brother might be wandering alone through life. She remembered the tantrums he would throw as a child when they didn't buy him the same doll as her. Her parents insisted that there was nothing for her to do in Mexico, that they'd inform her when Lumerso had returned home. Julieta never did miss her parents. She was the only Mexican that didn't return to her country during vacation time. The others were even given preferential treatment with finals so they might take off a few days before winter break. Julieta didn't care.

The first Christmas there she hated her family for leaving her alone in another country. Then, during the first summer, Josefina insisted she take some courses or that she travel through the continent; to make her point she draw attention to how many people would love to be in her place instead of begging her parents to fly her back to Mexico. She thought it was absurd that she didn't know to take advantage of her youth, instead of being bored in Third World lands. Josefina went as far as saying that if she were in Julieta's place, she wouldn't go back to Mexico for many years, just like her mother did.

Upon finishing high-school, Julieta received her diploma without any member of her family present to cheer for her at her graduation. Ignacio called her at the last minute to let her know they hadn't managed to put together the money to buy the tickets, but that they were all proud of her. Starting that fall, she'd start studying for a degree in Arts and Sciences, which guaranteed a good job in Mexico. Julieta was accepted in the University of Lausanne, despite not having gotten the best grades. Ignacio this time had nothing to do with that. Maybe one of the professors liked her, that was what Josefina thought. That summer Julieta worked at a camp for teenagers; it was the worst summer of her life.

Ignacio promised her that she'd be spending next Christmas with them in Mexico. It was enough to make her days a little brighter, excited for the summer to end. She was thinking of not returning to Switzerland. She didn't want to live there anymore or continue wasting time in studies that didn't please her. She hated not having a home. She didn't want to tell her parents for the time being. She thought about calling Lumerso and telling him her plans, but then she realized he might share the news with their parents before she arrived. She kept the secret until Christmas Eve.

She didn't remember the last time she'd talked to her mother. Every time she called Mexico, Jimena, Ignacio or Lumerso answered, but never Josefina.

Julieta kept putting on weight. When she turned nineteen, she went out with Victor, a boy of Swiss-Italian ancestry. He was a nice, young man with a strange sense of humor. He talked to Julieta in every language he knew, and she had to answer him in a different one. Julieta loathed that stupid game. European boys bored her, and their silly attempts at humor more so. A week later she stopped seeing him. She missed Cristina. She knew how to enjoy life in the boarding school. The dorm became a runway of boys from all the colleges and universities in Lausanne. Sometimes she got to hear Cristina having sex with even two in the same bed. Julieta, however, had followed Vivian's advice. Even though learning didn't come easy to her, she dedicated herself to studying. During the long winter days, she'd lock herself in the library, in her dorm, or any cleaning closet she found open. She didn't know why she liked small and dark places. Sometimes, during class, she'd become spellbound watching nothing, until she heard the professor interrupt her:

"What did you think of the class, Miss De la Torre?"

Julieta would feel shame and rush out of the classroom. She didn't manage to grow used to any of the jobs she took either. Sometimes she'd chat continuously with the students without regard for the language; other times, she remained locked inside her own bubble, in silence, with nothing to say. That was how she lost the job in the coffee shop, in the grocery store, and even as a ticket seller in the university theater.

The day she received the plane ticket from her father, Julieta went out to buy some gifts to take to the family. She bought red silk pajamas for Lumerso, a house-robe for her father and some earrings for her mother. She also bought gifts for Jimena. A day before the flight Julieta got her report card. She'd failed every subject. The faculty principal wanted to see her. She didn't care. She left.

On Christmas Eve, Julieta shared the news with Lumerso. She told him that she wasn't returning to Switzerland, and much less to the university. She stayed for a long time lying down on the couch, contemplating the baby booties her brother had just given her as a gift and a way to remember when they were babies. She thought of how much she adored Lumerso and how delicate he always was. When she heard her mother come downstairs to make coffee in the morning, she remembered how little they had in common. Julieta had always loved her, but her mother never tried to understand her. They were so alike, yet so different. Julieta went up to her bedroom without saying a thing. She slept for more than twelve hours. When she went to the dining room on Christmas Day, she found them all in the same positions as the previous night. She opened the fridge and served herself some eggnog she had prepared. Then she cut two slices of bread, filled them with ham, meat, and cheese; added mayonnaise and mustard. As Julieta began to eat, she glanced at her mother. Josefina usually judged her daughter for the way she fed herself. But this time she said nothing.

"Lumerso says you have something important to talk about," Ignacio said with much curiosity.

Julieta wanted to behead her brother with just a look. After finishing her sandwich, she spoke:

"I don't plan to keep studying, I want to release you of those expenses and those responsibilities."

Josefina's jaw seemed to drop onto the plate she had before her. She wanted to scream that between all the weight she had on her and what little education she got, she'd end up single for the rest of her life. Ignacio, however, could hardly contain the happiness he felt inside. He thought about investing in a seized apartment that the government was selling in Romita; that would be the best gift for his daughter. He told

Julieta that if that was what she wanted, he had no problem with it. He even told her that if she wanted to work, he could connect her with some friends in the public administration that could help her. Lumerso felt pride at being the only university student in the family. He looked at his cellphone that hadn't stopped vibrating and stepped out. Josefina said nothing. The silence with which she looked at her daughter was enough to know what she was thinking.

Lumerso no longer gave any explanations of when and at what time he came back since he and Julieta stopped talking to each other. Neither of them remembered the exact moment that actually happened.

The early morning that Lumerso didn't want to go up into their apartment, Julieta stole some pills her brother kept inside the nightstand. It wasn't the first time she did. Sometimes she took them to fall asleep; others, she saved them in a jar. When Lumerso went into the bar in Insurgentes Avenue, Julieta had taken a cocktail of a hundred pills, without knowing what each of them were for.

When he stepped out of the bar, Lumerso would have liked to have his sunglasses on his face. A dazzling blue sky wrapped the city; no cloud could be seen in miles. Lumerso tried not to think of how he must've smell or even looked. He walked until making it to the park in Romita. A few vendors were beginning to open their stalls. He returned to where he'd sat the previous night. Thought of Julieta, of the mistakes that, just like him, she too had made. The two of them lost everything: their parents, their careers, their dreams... and now they were completely alone. Without partners, without children, with nothing. They represented the end of the line. He remembered what Edgar told him: he had no one else, only her. He hurried to the apartment. He wanted to tell her how much he loved her, that she ought to go to the doctor, that he'd keep working so she'd live again. They could take away that horrible depression that didn't let her subsist. She didn't have to live like their mother; locked up in a void or in yesterday.

He made it to the fourth floor. He saw the apartment door ajar, perhaps his sister forgot to close it. The door to Julieta's bedroom was, like always, locked. He knocked several times but didn't get an answer. He couldn't hear her loud snoring. He went back to the entrance. Saw that the keys were on the floor. Concluded that Julieta got home but forgot to close the door. She'd done the same on other occasions. He kept banging on his sister's door but got no response. None of the keys opened the door. He went to the kitchen and found the stone of the mortar. He used it with all his strength on the lock until it broke. Lumerso couldn't believe what he was seeing. Julieta's body was lying lifeless on the bed. An old bedspread covered part of her body. The room stank of rotten food, piss, shit. Lumerso screamed like he did with his mother. He embraced Julieta, touched where blood had spilled from her lips, asked for forgiveness for not having helped her before. He thought of taking the rest of the pills in Julieta's hands. Threw them against the window. He wept until the neighbor from across the hall showed up with her husband. They both saw a reverse version of the depiction of Mary and Jesus in Michelangelo's sculpture, *La Pietà*: Lumerso was holding Julieta on the bed. The woman stared at Lumerso's bloodied hand. She ran to call the Emergency number. The ambulance and the police took an hour to arrive. Julieta had died eight hours before Lumerso arrived.

Chapter XXIII

Romita, 2019

Julieta's ashes were scattered at Playa del Carmen. She'd spoken so many times about that "infamous" trip to Cancun that Lumerso felt like he remembered the flight, the sea, the seashells, and starfishes she always talked about.

Jimena helped Lumerso vacate the Romita apartment. Nothing tied him to that place anymore.

Days earlier, after finishing with the closet, two wardrobes full of clothes, and shelves with shoes, Jimena stripped the bed. The sheets hadn't been changed in more than two months. A sour smell wafted from the mattress. Under the pillow, Julieta had placed a note that the forensic team hadn't seen. Jimena took it and without giving it a second thought dropped it in one of the pockets of her apron. Then she kept filling moving boxes in a messy way. She had no interest in carrying all of that to her home in the Buenos Aires neighborhood. The De la Torre family was approaching its end; however, she and her family were still alive. Her son told her several times that week that those kinds of tragedies only happened to rich people.

When they finished packing the kitchenware, Lumerso still didn't know what to do with Julieta's body at the time, which was at the morgue. He filled his backpack with a couple of sets of underwear, jeans and two t-shirts. He mentioned to Jimena that some people from the Charity House Niños de Dios would arrive in half an hour. Losing all his family was the worst thing that could have happened to him; her mother's only brother had moved with some *gringos* to San Miguel de Allende and he'd lost contact with him. He felt alone, hopeless, with no family by his side. The idea was to start a new life far away from any memory of that place and his family. He thought about having a new dog. He didn't care about his disease. He'd continue with the treatment he started at the clinic for the poorest. He didn't have to worry for his mother or Julieta anymore either. Likewise, the death of his sister taught him that things are fixed in this world and not in places high above. He gave Jimena a couple of bills. She placed her hand in the pocket of the apron. Handed him the note.

"I found it under one of Julieta's pillows," Jimena said matter of fact.

Lumerso put it away. Didn't give it any importance either. The paper had three lines written. The investigations freed Lumerso or other people from any kind of homicide charges. Julieta De la Torre simply suffered of chronic depression and decided to end her life. No one was to blame. Though an investigation had been started because drugs were involved; in Mexico, that would never get anywhere.

Before taking off, Lumerso hugged Jimena like he never did. He wanted to tell her that he always loved her, that he remembered every attention she had given him; especially, that she had returned his journal. Regardless, neither of them said a thing. Lumerso walked down the dark hallway without looking back.

After walking part of the Roma neighborhood, he walked into a *cafe* on the corner of España Park and Sonora Avenue. Lumerso felt that the world finally smiled again at him. A hard wind made the trees sway. Passersby walked with their dogs, while others jogged around the park. He turned to spit to get the dryness from his mouth out and, to his surprise, he found a box of condoms. He smiled. *Maybe it's a sign from a Divine being?* he wondered with a bit of a sense of humor. He picked the box making sure it was unused. Put it away inside his jacket.

He didn't know what to do or where to go. It had been some time since he stopped using the massage services app. The thought of having to explain to a new client the difference between an erotic massage and a relaxing one made him anxious. He needed to recharge, go out somewhere and forget once and for all about his own existence. He wanted to think of some other thing that wasn't sex or the horrible tragedies that took away his mother and Julieta. The sale of the apartment was necessary, no doubt about that. Julieta didn't write any last will; it was all the same to him, Lumerso didn't care at all about anything. It didn't matter if the government itself was the new owner. The flat at Romita had become a sad place flooded with bad memories.

Lumerso continued walking until he reached Mexico Park. A group of dogs rested by their owners. He thought that a German shepherd might be the new Oliver. An abandoned fountain glittered in the sun at three in the afternoon. A couple of birds burrowed their heads in a puddle of water. He observed an older man sitting on one of the benches. Eight dogs guarded him. Lumerso stared at his face. Lines of wrinkles crisscrossed his aged face. It was Santiago, Edgar's father. He sat by his side and at that instant Lumerso thought that he was as closest as he could be to his great love.

He waited in silence for a while. Lumerso didn't want to talk to him just yet; instead, he decided to study Santiago's face. He had the same nose, brows, and eyes as Edgar. A white beard covered part of his face.

Santiago talked to the dogs, he told them that it was time to leave. Lumerso finally said hello to him. Although they had only spoken a little in the past, Edgar's father recognized him immediately. One of the dogs barked. Lumerso caressed its head. The pup wanted to play, but with a serene voice Santiago calmed it.

"How are you doing, young man?" Santiago asked, still surprised of having run into his family's sworn enemy.

Lumerso held back his tears. He had confusing feelings. He thought of telling him that his sister had died, that his life was a mess, but decided it was better to be quiet. Wanted to hug him like he'd just done with Jimena. He was one of the persons he knew during his childhood. He asked the first thing that came to mind:

"How's Edgar? Where is he living?"

Those were some of the things he genuinely wanted to know. Lumerso tried calling him on the phone, but with no luck. He looked him up online, but he might as well have moved to Mars or Mercury.

Santiago looked at Lumerso's hopeless face. He knew beforehand that Magdalena sent Edgar abroad due to the love affair they had as teenagers. Though Edgar never told him anything, Santiago sensed for years how much he missed his best friend. Every time they met in Washington, D.C. it was the first thing he asked. Santiago didn't know what to tell him, other than life was no longer like before. The gay style was something Santiago wasn't clear on, though he did know the meaning of love. Without a pause, he calmly said what he'd repeated over the last six months:

"Edgar died in D.C."

The words of the man didn't settle well with what Lumerso thought he understood. How was it possible that he died before him? Life was unfair, it kept taking away the people he loved and the ones that were connected to him! Life made no sense. There was no God, there was no one that could control the hate he felt in that moment. He put his hand on Santiago's shoulder; he hugged him and told him that he'd like to walk back with him and help him with four of the dogs in his pack. Santiago agreed and gave him the smaller ones.

The backpack was heavy on him, his whole life in one bag.

While walking through Mexico Park, Lumerso remembered every second he and Edgar played together in the park, the morning walks with Grandma

Victoria and the uncomfortable talks with his father while they walked Oliver. When they were about to get home, Lumerso said he didn't want to go in, that he needed to process everything that was going on. But Santiago insisted Lumerso should go inside the house with him; he told him that the best medicine was talking, and who else could he do it with but with Edgar's best and oldest friend.

Upon opening the door, Lumerso felt Edgar's presence. He remembered the dining room table where they did their homework, and the kitchen where they ate every supper. He approached the TV set; it had been changed for an LED one.

When Santiago returned after taking the dogs to the backyard, he asked Lumerso if he wanted something stronger than a coffee. He showed him a bottle of tequila that someone gave Edgar as a gift at a Christmas party years ago and was still in its box. Lumerso opened it. He poured himself more than what would be considered "normal." Santiago chatted about Edgar marrying John in Washington, D.C., and how they then had a very private life. Almost never visited Mexico City. He began to lose weight. Lost his muscles. Everyone asked him if he was okay and he repeatedly answered the same: that it was an infection he'd gotten due to some fruits he ate in Chiapas. Santiago knew what he had. One day he went to his room and found him lying in his own feces, told him that it was best that he went to a hospital, or got admitted into one of those specialized clinics that were now everywhere. The following day he took the first flight and went back to Washington, D.C. Lumerso imagined the life that awaited him. The idea of finding himself alone was the worst that could happen to him. Now he couldn't even count on Jimena to look after him. He kept listening to Santiago until he said that three days later, he got a call from John letting him know Edgar had passed away that morning and that he didn't want his body returned to Mexico for burial. The news was devastating. Edgar's body was taken to the Poconos Mountains, in the state of Pennsylvania, where he and John had a cabin.

The bottle of tequila was already more than half empty. Lumerso filled the last two glasses, though not before toasting once more to Edgar. Santiago said that he could stay the night if he wanted to.

Edgar's room hadn't changed since the last time Lumerso was there. Two Spider-Man posters covered the wall on top of the desk. Some curtains with a childish print of sailboats hung slightly from the window. The clown lamp seemed to have stopped smiling. Lumerso lay down. The drinks didn't let him fall asleep. He wanted to find something that had the essence of Edgar; but regardless of how much he searched, he didn't find a thing. It was as if Edgar disappeared everything himself.

When Lumerso woke up it was past five in the morning. He was thirsty. He looked around and saw his backpack was where he left it, close to the TV set. Santiago was no longer there, he took the dogs on a walk at dawn. Lumerso drank some water and took off through the kitchen door. He didn't want to meet with the only good thing left of Edgar: his father.

The morning was crisp at that time although Lumerso knew that the beautiful sun rising was about to warm the day. Lumerso walked until he saw a coffee shop. As he tried to open the door, a manager signed to him they would be opening in a half hour.

Lumerso sat on the sidewalk to wait. He realized he had been in that place before. Opened the app to offer massages. Took the box of condoms and returned it to the street. He thought it was better for it to be picked up by some other idiot because he didn't need them anymore. He got several texts requiring his services.

When he went to pay for the coffee and the two donuts, the paper Jimena had given him fell to the floor.

"I'm sorry, Lumerso.
I'd like it for my ashes to be scattered
in the ocean at Playa del Carmen.
Julieta."

It was the note Julieta had left. He didn't have to worry about what to do with the ashes anymore. He'd call a funeral home to cremate the body. At least he'd have a project to do on the weekend. Perhaps he'd stay to live in Cancun and forget completely about Mexico, City. He opened a flight app to book a ticket.

Chapter XXIV

Playa del Carmen, 2019

After an argument with the taxi-driver, Lumerso got to Playa del Carmen. Having to pay eighteen hundred pesos for the trip from the airport would outrage anyone, it was almost the same amount as the plane ticket.

At first sight that place didn't impress him at all as he thought it would've. He felt like he'd arrived in another country. Nothing was even remotely Mexican: Outdoor European restaurants, music in English at high volume, white bodies showing off their new tans. It was another Miami Beach. The only thing missing was the *mariachis* singing in English. He didn't understand why Julieta had left that note. The ocean was beautiful, but the rest had nothing to do with the Playa del Carmen she remembered.

Lumerso rented a room in a seaside run by Italians. They got up and were loud like macaws long before the sun rose. The day after arriving Lumerso approached the ocean shore with a metal urn that contained what was left of Julieta. He smoked a couple of marijuana joints that the Italians sold him. Now everything made him laugh. He never smoked something that made him laugh so loudly. He suddenly understood why the Italians were so noisy in the morning. He walked by the seashore until finding a German man sunbathing with his ass in the air. Lumerso took off his shirt. The sun was beginning to heat things up. The German man watched him like he was the bait he was waiting for. Lumerso kept laughing about everything and anything. He introduced him to his sister: "Julieta De la Torre, dead December 17th, 2019; her last wish was that her ashes be scattered in these beaches." The man was dumbfounded, he had no idea what to say. He got away from Lumerso as quickly as he could.

The sun burned on Lumerso's back. The fishermen were starting to return. Lumerso tried to talk to Julieta. He told her that she was an idiot for taking her life and that he was upset; Julieta left him all alone in the world. Her presence at least helped him stay alive. Now, what was he going to do? Lock himself up in a room like her? Separate from the world completely?

He walked into the sea until the water reached his hips. A wave soaked the rest of his body. He submerged the urn until Julieta's ashes mixed with the ocean. He placed his face over the ashes that were beginning to float. With the face in the water he said amid bubbles: "Goodbye, my adored Julieta." Another wave took the remains of his sister.

When he was on the plane back to Mexico City, Lumerso noticed how peaceful the great metropolis looked. It seemed as if the *chilangos* were all sleeping. A line of cars with red lights looked from afar like a religious pilgrimage. Having been six days close to the sea had left him even more bewildered. Down there awaited him a world that he no longer understood. He located the old hotel of Mexico City; there, remarkably close, Chapultepec Park, then España, and finally Mexico Park. The place that saw him born; the place that saw him grow. However, the world was another; he was now another. Julieta's ashes made him reflect about his life. No one existed that would do the same for him. There was no point in living there in Cancun, in Mexico City, or in some other place. Anywhere was the same to him.

Upon arriving at the airport, he went outside and waited in line for a taxi. He didn't know what address to give the taxi-driver. Romita and Condesa were no longer home to him. Finally, it occurred to him to say: "La Casona in the Escandon neighborhood."

Final Chapter

Present

Lumerso lifts the backpack on his back and pulls out his cellphone to call Genaro. He tells him that he's thinking about going to La Casona, and that if he has some clients available, they could keep him company. Genaro replies that he's interested; but... better on another occasion, since today he doesn't have money.

"The money doesn't matter; what matters is pleasure," Lumerso goes on in an ambiguous tone.

Genaro likes the news, agrees to meet him with some friends in a couple of hours. After waiting for him in front of La Casona, Lumerso sees them arrive in an Uber, Genaro and three other men. The short one from the other time, a tall tanned one and another one: he's fat with a beer belly. The men go in, Genaro follows and finally Lumerso.

Lumerso cannot recognize himself when he sees himself in the entrance mirror. The last few months have transformed him. All of his feelings seem to have merged into one.

La Casona's foyer is packed with men. Some loom by the stairs, and others by the door. The receptionist can barely keep up. Some wait for lockers, others wander impatiently through the halls. They seem like locked-up hyenas wanting to get out of their cages, wanting to devour the first prey they find. Two men are kissing hard and heavy in a corner, it looks like they are trying to eat each other. Lumerso walks to the front of the line like Genaro orders him; to his surprise, he sees Erick. He finds him pale, tired... nonetheless, he still keeps that angelic look he's always had. He's chatting with a heavy man and an older one. Lumerso thinks he remembers them from the first time he was there. One of Genaro's men orders Lumerso to take off his shirt. He lowers his zipper. Lumerso whispers something to Erick, but he doesn't hear him. Lumerso goes into the bathroom, drinks water from the tap, gets naked, puts his clothes inside the backpack and throws everything in the trash. He has his wallet in the hand with a pair of hundred-dollar bills and his ID. He throws everything behind the toilet. He steps out of the bathroom bare: with no shoes, socks, or underwear. A tan accentuates even more his slim body. Lumerso's limp dick sways from side to side. The men look at him with lust. Some touch him, rub themselves against him. Genaro's group walks single line until they get to the basement. A wire curtain separates the dirty little room from the stairs. The place is dark. Genaro hands Lumerso a two hundred pesos bill. In the darkness Lumerso throws it to the floor. They start to tie him up. They hang him face-down. Lumerso closes his eyes. The fat one licks his back, Lumerso feels cold and indifferent. He feels no pleasure. Genaro puts three pills in his mouth. Then pushes them back with his fingers. Lumerso keeps having no reaction. The other licks his anus. Erick goes down to the basement, observes his friend through the iron chains of the curtain. The sadness in their eyes connects them. Neither of them wants to be there. Lumerso once again says something to Erick, but can't hear him. Erick runs back up the stairs and leaves La Casona. The fat one begins to penetrate Lumerso. The other gives him his dick to suck. Lumerso doesn't suck, he wants to swallow it. He wants to drown. To die. The man feels pleasure. A new one goes in, sees what's happening. It's the one with the mustache and the leather whip. Genaro gives him permission with only a look. He begins giving lashes to Lumerso. Now he climbs on him until he finds his ass hole. He penetrates him along with Genaro. Lumerso feels as if a saw were tearing him into pieces. Lumerso's penis begins having an erection. It's not pleasure that he's feeling. It's pain. It's the reaction to the pills Genaro pushed into him. His penis hurts. Everything hurts. He thinks of his mother, whom he hadn't remembered for so long. Remembers the times she'd go into his room, would kiss him and he pretended to sleep. And of Jimena when she prepared his breakfast before he went to school. Oliver waiting for him to give him a little more bacon. He'd like to see his father to ask for his forgiveness: *I'm sorry for having let you down, forgive me for being born gay. Forgive me...* Lumerso's tears cover his face. A bite on a nipple returns him to the moment. The man in leather bites his tits until they begin to bleed. Others hear what's going on with the man hanging and run to the basement. Genaro, amid so much pleasure, comes time and time again. He enjoys knowing how cheap these orgasms were to him. Lumerso feels palpitations in his heart. His head seems to spin. A line of men take turns to fuck him. A strong pressure in his chest continues without letting him breathe. He needs air. Someone gives him some poppers to smell. Lumerso doesn't stop smelling them. He's penetrated by everyone in the line; a line of sperm runs down the walls of Lumerso's anus and touches the floor. Lumerso feels a light over his body. His head falls. His body doesn't react. Another man wants to put his penis in his mouth. Lumerso no longer responds, he doesn't swallow anymore, he doesn't suck anymore, he's no longer there. A light is upon him. No one sees it. He doesn't feel it either. The short one keeps licking his hard cock. He doesn't know that Lumerso isn't there. Lumerso De la Torre has died.

Wilfredo finds the body hanging from one hand and both legs. Stains of blood and feces cover the floor. He thinks he remembers the guy from some other time. Upon releasing him, the lifeless body of Lumerso falls to the floor. Wilfredo doesn't scream. He picks up the bill. The price of death. It's his lucky day: he found a dead body along with a green bill. He doesn't climb the stairs like he used to either. He takes his cellphone and dials the owner. A listless voice answers the phone. Neither of the two seem to care about what happened to Lumerso. Two Lumersos are coexisting in that place now, the one that's lying on the ground, lifeless, and the one stuck in a corner, in the place that no one sees. He's awake; he can see but cannot go out; he's trapped between worlds. Lumerso gets up. Sees his body still with an erection. Wilfredo is standing close by; he's holding the broom. The lights are on as they wait for the arrival of the forensic team. Wilfredo finishes sweeping the floor. He doesn't use the mop. Lumerso follows Wilfredo, he notices his own lightness. He no longer feels remorse, guilt, nor pain. He passes by the foyer and finds the same men that were there the night before. He gets to the entrance door. Wants to go out, but cannot, he's trapped. there's no way he can get away from La Casona. He abandons it but doesn't seem to move from the same spot. Who's Lumerso now? An entity trapped in a call house. Will he have to live there eternally? Or is it only an instant? He climbs the stairs and finds a man asleep on the landing. Keeps walking but no one else is in the house. He observes the paramedics taking his body away while displaying cynical laughter on their faces. The place remains open. Lumerso wants to go up to the terrace, but the light blinds him, it doesn't let him go far. He curls up behind the armchair. Two men moan close to him. They enjoy themselves while Lumerso begins to understand he's stopped living.

Years go by and then one day La Casona is declared closed. Lumerso sees how they demolish the walls of the two houses. The collapse of one of the houses and then the other allows him to appreciate the burning light that tortured him before. He no longer wants to hide somewhere in the bathrooms, or the kitchen, or the dining rooms, or underneath the stairs to the basement. He no longer fears the light. The terrace was the first to be demolished. Some machines lift the two facades of the houses onto a truck. Lumerso observes how the streets begin to reappear. Street food vendors crowd together on the avenue. The vendor of *tamales* announces himself with a small chime, he no longer yells: "Oaxacan *tamales, tamales...*" Passersby walk upon the sidewalks. A wide sky seems to gift Lumerso a radiant sun. A quarter of moon begins to disappear on the other side of the city.

Like that, Lumerso stops remembering, ceases to be himself, stops being Lumerso De la Torre to continue in another time or space, beyond him, his world, us. Lumerso finds his freedom.

The characters in this novel are fictitious and do not hold any likeness with people living or dead.